PRAISE

"Intimate and compelling, *Love Like This* renders the subterranean longings of women and men in midlife and midstream—at the end of one way of being and at the beginning of the next. This complex and insightful story—about marriage, parenting, friendship, and rediscovering parts of yourself you thought were lost—lingers in the imagination long after you've read the last page."

SAMANTHA DUNN, AUTHOR OF *NOT BY ACCIDENT*

"Cynthia Newberry Martin brilliantly conveys the complexities of love and marriage. Her protagonist, Angelina, is torn between her love for her husband Will and her desire, now that they are empty nesters, to be alone and free to discover who she truly is and what she wants from her life. Martin masterfully depicts both the positive and negative aspects of Angelina's conflicting desires, and as a result even the smallest, most ordinary events in Angelina's life are packed with powerful drama. At one point a character tells her 'The world is full of wonder.' So is this book."

DAVID JAUSS, AUTHOR OF *GLOSSOLALIA:NEW & SELECTED STORIES*

ABOUT THE AUTHOR

Cynthia Newberry Martin's first novel, *Tidal Flats*, won the Gold Medal in Literary Fiction at the 2020 Independent Publisher Book Awards and the 14th Annual National Indie Excellence Award for Fiction. Her website features the How We Spend Our Days series, over a decade of essays by writers on their lives. She grew up in Atlanta and now lives in Columbus, Georgia, with her husband, and in Provincetown, Massachusetts, in a little house by the water. Her third novel, *The Art of Her Life*, will be published in June of 2023.

cynthianewberrymartin.com

CYNTHIA NEWBERRY MARTIN

LOVE

LIKE

THIS

www.vineleavespress.com

Print Edition
ISBN: 978-0-6454365-7-0
Published by Vine Leaves Press 2023

Cover design by Jessica Bell
Interior design by Amie McCracken

Grateful acknowledgement to George Saunders for permission to reprint his words as the epigraph.

 A catalogue record for this book is available from the National Library of Australia

To Cal with love

Stay open, forever, so open it hurts, and then open up some more, until the day you die, world without end, amen.

George Saunders, "The New Mecca"

CHAPTER 1

As if this Tuesday morning were the same as all the ones that had preceded it, Angelina stood at the kitchen sink while the man she'd loved for almost twenty-five years leaned over and kissed her goodbye. But instead of accompanying him to the back door, she kept a hand on the leaky faucet, her eyes on the North Georgia Mountains, and her ears on the anticipated click of the closing door. Then her hand slipped, and water burst from the faucet, spraying her black sweater.

Over the weekend, she and Will had deposited their youngest daughter at the University of Mississippi, where Iris would begin her new life, and they celebrated their empty nest by renting a one-room cottage at Lake Lanier. But at night, when she'd closed her eyes in that rustic wooden bed, her heart was holding onto this day when, for the first time in a lifetime, the house would be empty.

At the sink, she squirmed out of her wet sweater and dropped it on the kitchen floor.

Empty, not as in Cara was at school until three thirty but if she had study hall and then lunch, she might pop in during the middle of the day for an hour of TV and a tuna sandwich. Empty, not as in Livie would be at school and then volleyball until five thirty when she would want to know if Angelina had picked up the Orangina for the French club party. Empty, not as in Iris was in Atlanta for two nights with a friend. But *empty* empty. And Will would not be home before six thirty. Day after day until Thanksgiving, weekends excepted.

Angelina heard the garage door lumber up, the pause, and then its long-awaited landing. She began to count and was at twelve before she understood that she was counting just as she used to count to ensure that the baby was not only asleep but asleep for sure. She'd go all the way to a hundred before she dared rise from the rocker to make the transition to the crib. Even after so long, she could still remember what it had felt like to tiptoe out of the room, free of the tiny bundle for a minute, an hour, maybe two—as if a weight had been lifted from her body, as if it were too good to be true, as if it surely wouldn't last. Now her tiny bundles were all grown up and snugly tucked into the world—Cara in law school in Athens, Livie in Paris for fall semester abroad, and Iris in college in Mississippi. What Angelina had been longing for, she now had—a runway full of space with nothing in her path.

At a hundred she removed her watch and her rings, leaving them in the clay dish that stayed by the sink, the one with an *I* etched on the bottom—Iris had made it at camp. With wet hands, she turned to face the emptiness and off it went—shimmying across the wood floor and out into the hallway where she heard it swing around the banister, lunge up the steps, and fly through a triangle of coat hangers. She had made no plans for this moment. Intentionally. She was not going to *decide* to do anything. She wanted to see what would bubble up. Her fear was that there was nothing left to bubble.

She wiped her hands on the dishtowel Will had threaded through the handle of the drawer below the sink, the dishtowel that was so faded she could no longer remember its original color. Faded but soft.

Out the windows, the mountains that often disappeared in the distance today looked close enough to touch. At the pine breakfast table she and Will had bought at an estate sale right after they moved into this house, she kicked off her Nikes. The eighty-year-old woman who'd sold it to them said pine expanded and contracted to squeeze moisture from the center of the wood, that that's what made pine hard and gave it the ability to endure. The woman had no longer needed such a large table.

In the den, by Will's chair, Angelina took off her white shirt and watched it fall, watched one short sleeve catch in the crook of the leather recliner. Years and years of clothes—a build-up of clothes—had been holding her in place, weighing her down, obscuring her. Wife clothes and mother clothes. Aprons, cock-tail dresses, maternity jeans, chauffer hats, something-appro-priate, heels, boots, blouses, not-that-shirt-mom. In the dining room, in front of the double windows looking out at the quiet street, she peeled off first one thin sock and then the other. At the foot of the stairs, feeling lighter and picking up speed, she wiggled out of her loose pants. Halfway up, she wrenched her black sports bra over her head. At the top, she slid down her black underwear.

Naked, naked in an empty house.

She spun around and breathed out hard, over and over until she could settle down and focus on that tiny slice of the world she looked at every day—the sixteen worn steps, the shiny wooden handrail, the café-au-lait wall with the drawings of each of the girls at the age of five, the front door below with the four small square windows at the top and the rest of the world on the other side.

These hours from eight until six thirty—the heart of the day—were going to be her safety valve. Over the last few years, the feeling that she might explode—when *what's for supper* had risked blowing the lid off the pot—she had quieted with the words *the house is almost empty.*

She heard a noise and froze. There it went again. Ice falling in the icemaker. She folded onto the top step, which felt cold against her flesh. She gazed at her legs, at the blue veins that held red blood, at the misshapen toes. The ridges of the planks in the floor pinched. She rose.

At the end of the hall, the door to the phone room—a closet with a built-in desk—stood open. Angelina and Will had moved into this house and given the tiny room its name back before cordless phones. After that, it was where they installed the computer, back before laptops. Then it was the spot for the school supplies she bought each September. Now, Angelina didn't know what the room would be.

She drifted into their bedroom, its windows open to the warm September day. After drawing back the covers of the bed, she slid underneath. She used to sleep naked. And so had Will. But, according to Will, parents do not sleep naked.

Angelina raised the covers over her head and imagined the slick saltiness of waves crashing onto her skin, the tug of the ocean dragging her deeper and deeper. At the last moment, she would break free, kicking and thrashing her way toward the surface, piercing it, droplets dripping down her face, her eyes opening, sunlight sparkling all over her.

She stood. Everything in their room was in its place. That was Will. As well as her mother, she had to admit, and so her too. She extended her arms like a scarecrow, but she moved, twirling through the room—one, two, three. When she stopped, she felt as if she were still spinning, but as the spinning slowed, what was inside her started to settle. She could almost see the blank page that had existed years ago—before she chose to be a nurse, before she chose to be a wife, before she chose to be a mother. Before she understood that each choice would come with strings attached. And that each choice would rule out others.

On Will's night table sat his old-fashioned fake-wood alarm clock that he refused to part with because it still worked. Will was not a limitation exactly. She was glad he was there around the edges, a kind of frame. Instead of nothingness, Will. If she wanted to talk, he was the one she wanted to talk to. When he came home at night, she was glad to see him. She often sat on the front porch waiting for him. Perhaps she would wait for him tonight.

Something festive—that's what she needed. A mimosa. She would cut an orange wedge for the side of the glass. But instead of going straight downstairs, she went through the hall, rapping her knuckles against each closed door, listening to the emptiness that lay on the other side. Over the summer as Iris had packed for college, Angelina had organized pictures, cleaned out Cara's and Livie's rooms, stuffed boxes for the attic—reliving, as she did, the long-ago pleasures of miniature t-shirts, crinkled watercolor houses, and those wild-eyed birthday grins. Last week, after Will picked up the last suitcase and Iris ran out with one last shirt, still on a hanger, Angelina had shut the back door, content and satisfied. They would talk on the phone and come home for the holidays, but her day-to-day mothering was over.

With her hand just above the rail, she took one step down, then another. Her skin tingled. At the bottom, she darted to the windows in the dining room not knowing if she wanted someone to see her but knowing for sure she wanted to stand where someone could see her. And if she hadn't canceled the bug man, his dark eyes would have looked up just about now, and he would have stopped and stared. He would have wondered who this woman was—a woman who would stand in the window for all the world to see.

Without the bug man, it was she who was wondering who she was.

She had been twenty-five years old working as a nurse when she met Will, then twenty-six when they got married, twenty-seven when Cara was born, twenty-nine with Livie, thirty-one with Iris, and then she was forty-nine. *Now* she was forty-nine.

Angelina leaned forward to get as close to the glass as she could, pressing her face against its familiar surface. How little she could see—the grass, that was it. Or the children. Always another meal to cook, another dress to buy, another soccer game to watch, another call to answer. *Watch me, Mom.*

Until now.

Now, she could step back and take a wider view. She lifted her head from the pane, and as she did, a red truck passed in front of the house. She grabbed the rough drape, struggling to cover herself, and bolted to the foot of the stairs, snatching up her socks and black pants as she went. On the steps, she slowed only to gather her bra and underwear. Safely in her room, thinking not for the first time what a coward she was, she slammed the door.

On the second day, after the kiss by the sink and the click of the back door and the lumbering up and finally down, Angelina took a large Target bag out of the back of the hall closet and climbed the stairs. On their bedroom floor, she emptied the bag—plain M&Ms, peanut M&Ms, gum drops, a Snickers, Junior Mints, Good & Plenty, Reese's peanut butter cups, a Kit Kat, candy corn, a Butterfinger, Milk Duds, and sour gummies. She spread her offering around her in a circle, and her arms moved like the hands of a clock, her fingers dipping into each hour as she watched Sam Shepard and Susan Sarandon in the movie *Safe Passage* and wondered if all those Ss were just an accident. Angelina paused the DVD and took Susan's tone of voice—her get-out-of-the-way disregard for Sam—downstairs to the kitchen. As she poured Cheez-Its into a paper bowl, she wondered if that tone of voice was how you moved away from someone you loved.

Will had asked her out on a second date while they were still on their first; he had left her notes, stuck here and there, rough wide hearts above his name; he had wanted children and so had she; and he would do anything for her. Yet, if he could see her now, he would have frowned. Will didn't watch movies while it was light outside. He didn't eat between meals. He only used the bedroom for sleeping and sex. And he thought candy was for children, a childish thing to put away when you grew up. But her complaints about Will were trivial, childish in and of themselves. Life was about bigger things. Still, Angelina didn't know how to get to the bigger things.

The third morning, so thick with rain it was as if someone had pulled a gray curtain around the house, Will had to kiss her goodbye while she lay in the bed because that's where she stayed, curling her body into a ball and then stretching it in all the directions she could think of.

At six p.m. on Friday, the fourth day, she poured a glass of wine and filled the bath with bubbles, and that's where Will found her when he arrived home at six thirty.

Throughout the stormy weekend, as she and Will watched Georgia play Arkansas, talked to each of the girls on the phone, sat on the porch, and cooked steaks for supper, Angelina kept a brown bag of M&Ms tucked into the front pocket of her jeans, and as the spirit moved her, she popped a tiny treat of color into her mouth.

"M&Ms?" Will asked, cutting his eyes at the bag.

"Yes," she said.

●

Captivated by Monday's dancing rectangles of light, Angelina wandered from room to room following their traveling show. On Tuesday, a full week into her new life, she felt as if she could begin to unwrap herself—as if it were merely a question of drawing back layers of tissue. On Wednesday she felt that ache in her muscles and knew she wanted to feel blood racing through her veins again, which readied her for Thursday's thoughts of returning to nursing, thoughts that had surfaced several times over the summer. She had always been good at taking care of people, even before she had children. She exhaled, rolling her shoulders back. She didn't need to force things; she had plenty of time to allow herself to float to the top. The house would be hers until Thanksgiving.

●

On the morning of the second Friday, Angelina stood at the back door while Will got into his car and backed out. She continued to stand there as the garage door came down, sealing off the world and creating her own private universe where she turned and stepped lightly, as if to divine herself. In the bedroom, she stopped in front of her closet—full of clothes and well, full. Cluttered. Stuffed. Fatted.

Maybe she should start at the center and work her way to the outside. Or maybe this would be starting on the outside and working her way in? In any event, *in* she went.

First, she attempted to sort through her clothes while they hung in the small space of her closet, but she began to sweat. She felt suffocated and claustrophobic. So she gathered clumps of hanging clothes and laid them on the bed. She removed all her shoes, her stacks of sweaters, her baskets of umbrellas and purses, her suitcases, and her boxes and bags. She took everything out of the closet, every last belt and scarf. On the ladder, she cleaned the top shelf and the wooden rod. With a wet cloth, crawling on her hands and knees, she wiped the edge of the carpet next to the baseboard, creating a dirty black dust ball. She wiped the lower shelves and inside the drawers. She vacuumed and put up the vacuum.

Standing inside the clean closet, her sweaty clothes felt like weights. She stepped out, pulled off her clothes, and dropped them into the bathroom hamper. Naked again, this time in the small space of her empty closet, Angelina lay down on the carpet. She closed her eyes, breathed out, and was still. The only thing that moved was her chest, rising and falling as she inhaled the sweet smell of emptiness—an emptiness in which she was doing as she pleased so she could rediscover what pleased her.

She was thirsty. In the bathroom, the water fell rust-colored into the sink. After it cleared, she filled her glass, taking a sip of the earthy-tasting water on her way back to the closet, where she sat, crossed her legs, and placed the glass in front of her. Instead of still, she became uncomfortable. Reaching for the glass, her heart constricted and took off. Little pinpricks ran up and down her body. She was thirstier now than before. Out of the depths of where she didn't know, came a memory from the first month they were married. As they sat side by side in their small den watching the Braves, she had turned to Will and said, "Would you get me a glass of water?"

She hadn't known it then—in fact she hadn't known it until this second—but what happened after she asked for that glass of water changed who she was in the world. It caused a crack in something she'd been sure of.

"You don't do that," Will had said, frowning, his face hard.

"You don't do what?" she asked.

"When two people are equally able to get something, you don't ask the other person to get the thing for you. It's not appropriate."

Sure you did. Where she came from, they did it all the time. For each other.

He was firm and he was positive. "It's not appropriate."

Her face had turned red, and her throat had dried up. She couldn't speak. And then she'd disappeared, her true inappropriate self headed for the hills and into hiding. As Will unveiled rule after rule, "Oh," was what she said, instead of "I don't think so," or "Not in my world," or "Let's talk about this." True, he had bullied her, but she had dissolved.

Over the years, what she told herself was that marriage required compromise, and compromise required that people soften their edges. But softening her edges meant she was less herself.

Angelina got up from the closet floor, accidentally knocking the glass, but instead of quickly righting it, she just stood there, watching the water darken the carpet. Then she stepped over the empty glass and the flooded carpet. After all, it was just water.

On a chair, in a sealed plastic bag, she found the new exercise clothes she'd ordered the week before—form-fitting black Lycra pants that enabled her to move and a long-sleeved white top that hugged her body and ended with bell-bottom sleeves.

In the bathroom, wearing her new clothes, she looked in the mirror and could see the extra roll that had recently appeared around her middle. She twisted to see the rear view. There was her butt—in plain sight. She reached for the hem of her shirt to pull it off over her head but instead, she dropped her arms. That roll was her, as was the butt. She wanted to make peace with them, not banish them from sight.

As she passed her closet door, she noticed the glass still lying on its side and grabbed a towel, which she laid over the spill. It was after three, and she was hungry—she'd never stopped for lunch—*and* she wanted to put her clothes back in the closet before Will got home. But on all fours, pressing the towel to absorb the water, she was so close to the carpet. Instead of going to the kitchen or putting things back where they had been, she lay down on top of the towel to give some thought to what she wanted to keep and what she wanted to discard.

CHAPTER 2

"This is going to be great," Will said, out loud to himself as he opened the back door and stepped into the kitchen.

Where in the world was Angelina?

Shutting the door with his back, he leaned against it, hugging his computer case to his chest. "Angelina?" he called out.

Left to right—breakfast table, opening to the den, sink where Angelina was usually standing, door to the dining room, desk right beside him—he drank it all in as if he'd been thirsty for it and hadn't even known. But sure he had. This was what he'd wanted for ages.

"Angelina?" he said again. And there she was, peeking her head in from the den. "I didn't see you. Where were you?"

"What are you doing here?"

"I live here," he said, and he tossed his case on the desk by the phone where it knocked into the mug of pens and pencils.

"Are you okay?"

Will loosened his already-loose tie and paced in a small circle. He needed to say this just right. Then he stopped short. "I was fired."

"You were fired?"

"That's right," he said, corralling pens and pencils. "I told Harry I didn't like the way things were changing. He said retirement was an option and suggested I take it."

He looked at her and waited. Why didn't she say something and why was she just standing there in the middle of the doorway?

"Twenty-five years at the Water Works," he said. "And just like that, I'm not going back." He picked up a piece of mail. "Can you believe it?"

"No," she said.

This wasn't going as he'd pictured it in his head. In fact, it really did feel as if he wasn't supposed to be in his own house. Well, of course, he wasn't. He was supposed to be at work. Instead, he was standing here not telling his wife the truth. Years ago, right when it became the truth, he should have told her. And today, after Harry had offered him the "opportunity" to travel again, Will had acted so badly. Not at all like himself. All he ever wanted to do when he grew up was the right thing. Ever since third grade when his father had left him and his mother. That's when he learned how important doing the right thing was.

"I was about to take a shower," she said, rubbing her chest. "I'll be right back."

"Fine," he said. And then under his breath, "Just fine." He moved to the windows, but all he saw was a replay of the scene at the office. Harry would kill to travel, he'd said. Kill to work until he fell over. Phyllis had big plans for him when he retired, plans that included babysitting the grandkids and helping her in the yard, plans he wanted none of.

Will turned to face the empty doorway where Angelina had stood. She was acting odd again. Like those tears in Mississippi. One minute everything was fine. They were hugging Iris goodbye. The next thing he knew, Angelina was bawling and unable to speak. He got them out of there as fast as he could, but she kept crying. After forty-five minutes, he finally thought to stop at a liquor store for a bottle of wine. He'd grabbed some plastic cups and a bag of ice, and set up a bar in the trunk, embedding the bag of ice in an old towel. Wine with ice—which had reminded him of the first thing he'd done for her, the night they met at a mutual friend's wedding. That time it had been beer instead of wine. "I've never had ice in a beer before," she'd said, and smiled. And that was that.

What would Will do at home, Harry had asked. Putter around the house? Spend all day with Angelina? Yes, Will thought. And yes.

CHAPTER 3

Angelina continued to rub her chest, the place over her heart, which felt not as if her heart were breaking but as if it were splitting in two. At the top of the steps, she paused. But she didn't go back to the kitchen; she continued to the bedroom. Where it looked as if her closet had exploded. Clothes lay on the bed, in piles on the floor, and across the chest of drawers. She was supposed to have had two more hours before Will got home. She picked her way through the debris, stopping at her closet to look for something—but her closet was empty except for a towel and a glass. So she kept going, closing the bathroom door behind her.

To make good on her claim, she started the shower. When she peeled off the new clothes, her skin felt raw, and she just stood there, staring at the small black and white pile on the floor. Then she grabbed it up and stuffed it in the hamper, pushing and pushing, burying her new clothes along with the self she'd been holding onto for a very long time, that she was just catching hold of again.

In the shower, she leaned her head against the tile wall and let the water—Will's water—pelt her back. Then she turned to watch it run over her fingers. When she felt it pooling around her feet, she made a fist and hit the wall. The drain was stopped up again.

Downstairs, Will was sizzling onions in the skillet. Everywhere she looked, nicked counters and outdated appliances. A package of ground beef lay ripped open, a red spiral escaping from the plastic wrap.

"You know, one is the loneliest number," he said, looking up and smiling.

"Two can be as bad as one," she said. But she was tired of her lines.

"It's the loneliest number since the number one," he said. Then he opened his arms, and she fell in. It was what she did, what she was supposed to do. Any other response would have required words she didn't yet have.

They stood wrapped together in the kitchen. Song lyrics stayed with you for so long. Longer than the people you'd listened to the songs with. The year she first sang to "One" in the dark cafeteria, she'd loved the boy with the half-smile who slung his bangs out of his eyes. For the dance, she'd gone on a peanut butter and jelly diet and lost five pounds in a week. She'd worn a short little blue and white dress with bell-bottom sleeves and an empire waist. Perhaps songs should disappear along with the people with whom you had loved them.

As she and Will drew apart, she said, "I'm sorry about your job."

He shrugged, then opened the fridge, lining up the different varieties of milk on the top shelf before he took out the leftover tomatoes.

Will was perhaps more handsome now than when she'd first met him, the flecks of gray in his black hair adding depth—a rugged layer—to his face. He usually told people he was six feet tall, which was stretching things by at least an inch, and his body these days gave her more to hold on to. But when he turned away from the fridge, he looked smaller than usual. His face was pale, and he still had on his dark glasses.

Angelina had counted on the empty house, but Will must have counted on work. Their vulnerability now sailed her back to Will's first rainy day on the job. He had dripped into this very kitchen in the gray jacket she'd bought to protect him while he worked. Water-resistant, he'd said. Not waterproof. She'd helped him out of his clothes right here. She'd kissed the crook of his neck.

"I didn't have much of an appetite for lunch," he said, stirring the onions. "I thought I'd fix spaghetti if that's okay. It didn't look like you had anything planned."

Her face heated up, and she snatched two wine glasses from the cabinet. If he'd come home at his usual time, she would have had something planned because Will, as she was well aware, required that supper be planned. If it were just her, she'd cut a piece of cheese, munch on a few chips. At night she didn't want a meal.

Back in the fridge, he was now lining up the juices on the other side of the shelf.

"Excuse me," she said, as she stretched around him for the wine.

"Oh, sorry, I'm done," he said. "You don't know why there was a spoon in front of the garage doors, do you?"

She shook her head.

"Well, I brought it in," he said. "And stuck it in the dishwasher."

Angelina heard the plop of ground beef into the skillet behind her over the sound of wine filling their glasses in front of her. She left Will's full glass beside the giant bottle of pinot grigio. In the den, from where it lay draped across a chair, she scooped up what had become her jacket after they could afford to buy Will one that was waterproof. "See you outside."

"Right behind you," he said, and she paused, lifting her head, before pushing open the porch door.

●

On the porch, she shivered, her thoughts darting from Will to her mother, who had always been right behind her too. Angelina sat in the rocker farthest from the door and next to the small end table Will had been making when they met, the table that was now scarred by splintered wood and watermarks. She placed her jacket on the arm of the chair between her and the rest of the porch.

Five rocking chairs where there used to be only two.

Will appeared. "We can count on the view, can't we?" he said.

Their small house sat high in the Blue Ridge Mountains of North Georgia, and the back looked north over rolling hills. The light was changing, evening beginning. A thick layer of smoky orange obscured the mountains.

"You know," he said, "people drive from all around to see what we have right here." He ran his fingers down the screen she usually didn't see. A swoosh of birds flew by fast and close.

Angelina shivered again. When she was little, every time she left the house, her mother, who did not go out, would say, "Don't pick up any dead birds." Angelina had known birds flew in the sky, and she assumed that was where the dead ones would come from too. She could still see that brown bird with his alligator eyes and his tail feathers sticking up behind him who made nests in their garage. He would swoosh through, narrowly missing her head, then watch as she got in her father's car. Like he wanted something from her. After he left his gooey white crap on her favorite Beatles sweatshirt, she began to hover by the back door instead of busting through it. Even now, she could remember the scratchy, cold feeling of pressing her face against the metal, how she'd stood there for hours, trapped, her hand around the slim rusted knob, rubbing her nose up and down and around in circles on the screen. That was when her father had explained her mother's disease.

"It's not that she's afraid to go out," he'd said.

"It's not?"

"It's that she's afraid of being afraid. That feeling of panic. It's not about what's out there."

Her father had given her an umbrella and told her that would keep her safe, and for years, she wouldn't go anywhere without one. Although these days she no longer had to rely on an open umbrella to feel safe, she often clutched a closed one or scanned for birds.

"Did you hear anything from the girls today?" Will asked.

From the distant hills to the shape of her husband on the porch. His question was an offering—giving her time to adjust to his news. "Nothing from Cara," she said. "Livie emailed a picture— not of her but of a field of sunflowers outside of Paris..."

"What was she doing *outside* of Paris?"

"And Iris called wanting to buy some clothes for Rush."

"How is Rush different from college?" he asked, coming toward her, touching her leg as he sat down beside her. His hand was wide, his fingernails bitten unevenly to below the quick. "Hard to believe I'm not a water doc anymore."

She almost smiled hearing the name Cara had given him years ago when she'd sat at the kitchen table with her homework asking each of them *what they did*. Angelina had defended her claim that she was a nurse.

"I don't have to be doing it now to be one," she'd said.

Will hadn't fared much better. "What do you mean, *engineer?*" Cara asked. "You work on a train?" Then Will had said something about working with water. "With water?" He told her he tested it to make sure it wouldn't make people sick. Cara started writing then. Angelina passed behind her putting a stack of placemats and plates on the table. *Water docter,* she had written in her large scrawl.

"Iris seemed happy, didn't she?" Angelina said. "At Ole Miss." But taking the last one to college was different. It was the end of something.

"Three reasonably self-sufficient daughters," he said, "launched into the world." And he raised his glass. "To us."

She nodded her glass in his direction.

But he leaned toward her, reaching his glass until it clinked on hers. The glasses always had to touch.

She looked toward the mountains, taking a sip. "This moment is farther than I could ever see."

"Not me," he said.

"I mean, when I fell in love with you," she said, "I could foresee little children—even maybe three of them. But I never saw how they would take over our lives and then that one day in a galaxy far away, we might get those lives back."

"I could always see this moment," Will said. "I can already see us with grandchildren." He laughed.

She didn't.

What Angelina could see was maybe running again. She hadn't run since college, but she used to run. Or maybe working a half-day at the hospital. Or planning a trip for them to Paris. Or reading the novel about the woman at the shore. Or cooking together like Will had always wanted to, but for fun, not because there had to be dinner. And there would be no more angry teen-agers. No away games. No pressure. They could talk all night, maybe even skipping dinner because she wanted to talk and he wanted to listen.

"I'm sorry I've upset things," Will said. "Upset you."

"Me?"

"Aren't you upset?" he asked.

"But you're the one who lost your job." She had no right to be upset. She wanted to think of him. But she had put so much hope in the empty house, and her tears spilled out.

He got up, crouched in front of her, and put his arms around her. His neck always had the lemony-geranium fresh smell of his Old Spice deodorant.

She forced a breath and then sat up. "I should be comforting you," she said, as she wiped the corners of her eyes with the sleeve of the jacket beside her.

"I don't need comforting," he said.

So she looked over him, past him to the screen and through to the trees. Of course, trees were good at change. They did it every year.

With his hands on his knees, he stood, like a rusty lawn chair being extended and more slowly than she suspected was neces-sary. He still had on his good clothes. Brown loafers, khaki pants, a long-sleeve button-down shirt, and a tie—his uniform for the past five years since he'd stopped working in the field.

Will was the kind of man who did everything *beforehand*, as if that were some sort of virtue. Usually after work, he went right up to change. Then he turned down the comforter. When he came back downstairs, if he were cooking or she wasn't, he would arrange the food on the counter that he would use later for dinner. Then he would turn on the TV. At least when he was watching TV, he wasn't watching her.

The wind ran through the trees.

"I've thought about going back to nursing," she said. "You know I've kept up my certification." That had always been their contingency plan.

"Angel, money isn't a problem. We've saved. And I got the retirement package. Neither of us needs to work. We're good." He rubbed the foot of the wine glass on his cheek as if scratching an itch.

"We're good?"

"I planned for retirement."

Of course he had.

Angelina stood and put her hand on the screen. Then she turned to look at her husband who was supposed to go to work Monday through Friday from eight a.m. until six thirty p.m. Maybe he hadn't changed his clothes because this was the last time he would wear them. "What are you going to do now?" she asked.

Will raised his hands to the side as if he were asking the congregation to rise. Then he laughed. "I think we should get naked and have sex."

She laughed too, finally. Finally. "That's always your solution," she said, and then, "I'm going to need more wine."

CHAPTER 4

The next morning, Angelina came downstairs to find Will reading the paper in his pajama pants, robe, and slippers. Usually, even on the weekends, he would throw on old khakis and, if it were cold, a maroon sweatshirt that advertised one of the girls' softball teams, though she couldn't remember which girl.

Picking up his coffee mug, he said, "I've worked with water long enough," as if they were in the middle of a conversation.

She kept going into the kitchen and turned on the electric kettle. Into her green mug, a tea bag. But he came to exactly where she was standing in the kitchen.

"I'm tired of things slipping through my fingers," he said. "I'm tired of waiting for that little bit of sediment to settle in the bottom of the beaker. I want to work with something solid."

"I didn't know you were so unhappy," she said, moving away from the kettle while it heated and around the table to the windows, but she couldn't see anything through the fog.

"Angel, I wasn't *so* unhappy. But I want to make things again. If it's okay, I'm going to set up a workroom in the basement?"

The basement. Right here in this house. With her every minute of every day. *What are you doing? Where are you going? What do you want for lunch?*

"*Is* it okay?"

"Of course," she said. Why did he always phrase things to require something of her?

"And I might finally get those wind chimes," he said.

Angelina spent the day stuffing her clothes back in the closet, walking up and down every aisle of the grocery store, and sitting in her car to eat a late lunch. Will at home seemed like a wall she couldn't get over or find a way around.

That evening, from where she sat in the den, all she could see out the window was gray—no fading light, just gray, then dark. The Braves were playing, and she opened her book or what remained of the book. Her best friend Kate had given her Jim Harrison's *The Woman Lit by Fireflies* but ripped out the first two stories, leaving only the title story, saying she wanted Angelina to get right to the point.

"You tore the book apart?" Angelina had asked.

Kate was trying to persuade her that she didn't need to spend time in an empty house, that she needed to get *out* of the house. Which is what Angelina used to tell her mother before Angelina understood how sick her mother was.

"Nothing says I care more than mutilating a book," Kate had said, also handing Angelina a basket with a card—*Happy wide-open spaces of you.* In the basket Angelina found rosemary bath oil, an over-sized bag of bite-sized Snickers, and a tiny travel vibrator in a blue silk drawstring pouch.

Last night, with Will snoring beside her, she'd finished a collection by Ellen Gilchrist. Angelina wanted to be one of the

34

women in those stories. A woman who would do anything—
drive all night to Mexico, rob a bar, set off like in a dream, walk
into the ocean to die. She'd been fired up, not ready to sleep. So
she'd eased out of bed to find the book Kate had given her, finally
discovering the basket underneath one of her black dresses. On
page one, the firefly woman was driving with a headache to
avoid having to read to her husband, which is what he required
when *he* drove. Angelina had gone quiet inside. She'd closed the
piece of book, placed it on the floor, and turned out the light.

"Leave him in," Will said, and then he cleared his throat.

Take him out, Angelina thought.

Instead of reading, she was now peeling off the uneven edges
of the interior binding where Kate had torn out the other pages.
She was building a little pile of ecru paper and glue slivers that
reminded her of something, but she wasn't sure what.

"Awe, come on," Will said, clearing his throat again. "Give the
guy a chance."

She thrust the book in her purse and snatched up the purse.

"Where are you going?" Will asked, the newspaper crinkling
as he turned a page.

"To drive around," she said loud enough for him to hear as
she left by the back door, which she didn't exactly slam but shut
with perhaps too much force for a clean getaway. She started her
Volvo and then checked behind her, watching the garage door
struggle up. As she faced forward, there was Will. She breathed
out and let her window down part way.

"You never go anywhere at night," he said.

"Now I do," she said and backed up.

But he stood there, his hands in his pockets.

She lowered the window the rest of the way and leaned her
head out. "I'll be back in an hour."

At that, he went back inside, and she pushed the button to lower the garage door.

After twenty-two years of taking care of children, all the alone she got was nine days. And that wasn't enough. Not nearly enough.

CHAPTER 5

It had been two weeks since Black Friday, the day Will had come home for good. The first week, Angelina took a refresher course at North Georgia Hospital, and the second she did the HomeHealthCare training in the downtown Blue Ridge building that housed their office. Now Angelina had her first patient. Lucy G. Craft, a total hip. But Lucy had no phone. Angelina sat in a swivel chair at a borrowed desk, inhaling patchouli and staring at the yellow-painted cement-block walls. There had to be a phone number somewhere, and she opened the thick file again.

"Is this John Craft?" she asked. "Lucy Craft's son?"

"John Milton," he replied in a deep, growly voice. "John Milton Craft."

Moments later, on the way to her car, safe under a plain black umbrella, Angelina paused in the dusky rain. Despite the upheaval of the last few weeks, everything around her looked the same. She glanced at the ridge for which the town was named and where their house and Will sat waiting for her. Nothing but a giant bluish-green wall. On Main Street, the Oglethorpe Oaks looked greener than ever. Over the summer, it had been strange to think of nursing, strange to imagine opening that door again, Cara now the age Angelina had been when she'd first worked as a nurse. On a second glance at the ridge, she found its uneven edge, where here and there a single tree jutted out and separated itself from the others.

At the beginning of the next week, Angelina looked for Lucy's trailer, her first marker a convenience store on Victory Drive. A quarter of a mile later, she was supposed to see three single-wides lined up in a row off to the right. As she passed the convenience store, what looked like a plastic shield for a pay phone lay busted on the ground next to an overflowing trashcan.

Spotting the three dull white trailers made her realize that John Milton Craft had not told her which one Lucy lived in. There didn't seem to be a driveway either, and Angelina cringed as she bumped over the curb, the gravel popping the underside of the car. She parked in front of the first trailer she came to—rust-striped and the most run-down of the three, with a #1 colored on a piece of paper and masking-taped to the door. Rain must have caused the #1 to dribble down the paper, but today was an early October day with a crispness in the air that made the sun warming the dashboard a welcome stranger.

Her notes said something about a Rottweiler, and she glanced at the passenger seat. The black and silver canister of pepper spray Will had given her last week lay next to the tiny new umbrella she'd bought for herself—sky blue. After opening the car door, she opened the umbrella, the tiny metal prongs scaffolding for a false but safer sky. Cars whizzed by on her left. Empty plastic bags littered the tree branches and undersized shrubs. Angelina hurried the few steps to the cement block that served as a doorstep, wondering if it came with the trailer.

When she knocked, she heard barking. An aluminum door made sense, though. It would be stupid to have a real door on a fake house.

"I'm coming. I'm...coming."

"Will you make sure the dog is tied up?" Angelina shouted over the barking.

As the door opened a crack, a voice said, "Are you afraid of Little Old Lady?" And then there were two tiny eyes. "Is it raining?"

"Not at the moment," Angelina said, looking down for the Rottweiler that was nowhere to be seen and had stopped barking. The door opened all the way.

A giant human square is what four-feet nine-and-a-half inches and 210 pounds looked like. If Angelina were that fat, she'd probably have high blood pressure, high cholesterol, diabetes, and depression, too. No wonder the woman needed her hip replaced. No wonder she was having unexplained abdominal pain. At two weeks post-op, Angelina wondered if that was considered a complication or a new condition. Antibiotics and laxatives had been prescribed.

"You the nurse?"

"Yes, ma'am." Angelina had forgotten she might not be at the right trailer, but now she guessed she was. "You're Lucy G. Craft?"

"That's me," the woman said, wheeling her walker around and away from the door.

Angelina collapsed her umbrella and stepped inside. Normally, she liked the smell of bacon.

A card table sat in a corner between a window and a little piece of wall that separated the kitchen from the rest of the room. Lucy squeezed into a metal folding chair angled into the corner itself. She leaned her head back against the wall and exhaled.

Angelina sat in the other chair and started to put her purse on the floor, but after looking at the dirty linoleum, kept it in her lap. A purple plastic bucket, like for kids at the beach, and full to the top with medicine bottles, sat between them on the table. Angelina used the edge of her hand to wipe an area in front of her free of crumbs and dust, but the crumbs stuck to a sticky spot, then some of the stickiness stuck to her hand, which she wiped on the rim of the table, but she just kept picking up debris. *Move on*, she told herself.

Angelina put the chart down, angled to the left. Now she smelled something else, something under the bacon, something like...she couldn't say what it was like, but it was a bad smell. She dug in her purse for a pen. "Okay," she said. "May I call you Lucy?"

"I don't see why not."

Angelina smiled. "Lucy, my name is Angelina."

"Of course it is," Lucy said, pushing a strand of greasy gray-black hair behind her ear.

Angelina smiled again.

Lucy didn't.

"Okay," Angelina said. "Let's just get you admitted and then we'll get the history out of the way."

"But they said..."

"I don't have to take you anywhere. It just means I'm admitting you into the HomeHealthCare system. It's really more of a book-keeping or computer thing. Later you'll be discharged too. After four weeks. That's what Medicaid is paying for. Four weeks of in-home care. Is your full name Lucille?" Angelina swatted at a fly.

"Lucy."

"Your birth date is April 1, 1960?" Angelina thought Lucy looked older.

But Lucy nodded.

"I was born in 1960 too," Angelina said. "In January. We're the same age."

Lucy's mouth made a squeak as it opened wide in a yawn. Angelina looked away, back down at her papers.

"Okay, obviously I have your address. Can you receive mail here?" Jeez, she was so damn judgmental. Over the door, where this future mail might come in, were two butcher knives forming an X. Angelina shook her head slightly to clear the image.

Lucy gave her a post office box, confirmed the Medicaid information, and without reading anything, signed and put initials where Angelina asked her to. Now for Lucy's weight. Angelina put the scale she'd brought on the floor. Lucy leaned on the table to stand and did not remove the sweater that did not fit or her dirty slippers. 216 pounds. Six more since the surgery. The tape measure confirmed her height.

To take her pulse, Angelina placed two fingers on Lucy's wrist and looked away. Magazine photographs of Michelangelo's *David*, his *Pietà*, and various shots of the Sistine Chapel, including *The Creation of Adam* and lots of scaffolding and men working with cloths, were taped to the wall above the table. Several yellowed tape marks lined the torn edges. The fly landed on the table. She took Lucy's temperature and blood pressure and completed the rest of the physical.

After taking Lucy's history, which took over an hour with all the complaints about headaches and stomachaches, the explanations, the remembering, the searching for documents, and then the corrections, Angelina said, "All that's left is the medication."

"Aren't you going to ask me about my dreams?"

"Nurses don't normally ask that."

"I thought you might, though."

"Why?"

"Just did."

Angelina looked at Lucy. "Let's start at the top of this medication list and work our way down. First, are you still taking the Dilantin?"

Lucy tipped the purple bucket toward her. "Which one is that?"

Angelina put her pen down and dumped the bottles onto the middle of the table. She began to group them in families according to purpose. Halfway through, Little Old Lady barked and the door opened and a big black bear came in. At least that was Angelina's first thought, but of course it wasn't a bear. It was a man—in a black t-shirt, loose over a slight paunch—whose large arms, in addition to his head, were covered in long black hair that took off in all directions. His head hovered dangerously close to the ceiling. She looked at Lucy and picked up some resemblance—the shape of the face maybe, both with wide foreheads and narrow chins. This must be the son she had talked to. The one pregnancy at the age of seventeen—the live birth—she had just listed on Lucy's chart. That made him younger than he looked—thirty-two. Angelina expected to be introduced. All she got, though, was a nod before he headed to the back. Ten seconds later, without the sound of a door shutting, she heard a thudding stream of pee, followed by the short blast of a fart, and then the flush of a toilet. She could not imagine living with someone in such close quarters.

The bear thundered into the kitchen, yawned loudly, and opened the fridge. He picked up a red flyswatter and slapped it against the countertop.

Angelina glanced at Lucy, who had her eyes on the man and her finger scratching her head, working at a particular spot.

Then there was the pop of what Angelina expected to be a can of Schlitz Malt Liquor, the giant size, but turned out to be a large V-8. The man said, in that gruff voice, "When you're done with her, feed the dog."

Angelina wasn't sure if he were speaking to Lucy or to her.

Then he banged out the door.

"In school, they wanted him to be Lil' Abner, but he wanted to paint sets. His teachers would say how he always had his head in the clouds. I was so proud. And now he paints signs on billboards." Lucy smiled for the first time. Then she looked around the trailer, her eyes settling on the door. "I forgot to take my blood pressure medicine."

Angelina had been good at memory games when she was a child, and she went straight to the right bottle. She tipped one pill into Lucy's outstretched hand, her fingers wiggling like tiny animals. When Lucy leaned on the table to stand, most of the bottles fell over. One by one, Angelina straightened them. A few seconds later, she looked up to see Lucy pondering a selection of used glasses on the counter and choosing one with an inch of red liquid in it.

"Another maggot," Lucy said, looking into the sink.

Angelina stood. During the summer, she and Will had watched a *60 Minutes* episode on alternative methods of healing, one of which involved maggots, but she'd never seen a live one before.

"I open the door and launch 'em into the bushes, and the next day they're back again."

Angelina found a light switch and flipped it, but nothing happened.

"Burned out," Lucy said, picking up a fork from the counter and scooping, not spearing, what Angelina could see now was a gooey little worm-like thing. Again, Angelina smelled the something-besides-bacon foul smell. She sniffed in various directions, including toward Lucy while Lucy was busy with the maggot, but the odor did not seem to get stronger or weaker.

Lucy, the maggot, and the walker set out for the door.

She should tell her to find out where the maggots were coming from. "You know—"

"Damn."

"What?" Angelina asked.

"Dropped the little bugger."

No way could Lucy bend over. Nor was she supposed to.

"I guess he'll find his way back to the sink after a while," Lucy said.

"Maybe I can find him," Angelina said. She took the fork from Lucy and bent to the floor. The gooey thing was wiggling toward a dirty sock. Angelina got the tines underneath him and carefully raised the fork, holding it at arm's length and wishing her arm were longer. With her left hand, she opened the door and slung the maggot in the direction of the only bush she saw. She closed the door and breathed out.

Lucy was standing behind her, watching.

Angelina smiled. "Did you take your pill?"

Lucy shrugged.

Angelina found the blue pill by the edge of the sink.

"You're good," Lucy said.

Angelina had to admit she was finding herself oddly suited to Lucy's needs.

After dropping the pill on her thick, pasty tongue, Lucy slugged some of the rosy liquid and scooped her head forward as if that would help the pill go down. "It's gone," she said, extracting a saltine from an open pack on the counter and stuffing it in her mouth. As she chewed, she appeared to be rolling the gummy paste around the inside of her mouth. Then she reached for a cartoon jelly glass with about an inch of golden liquid in it and gulped it all. "That's better," Lucy said.

Angelina had been holding her breath again and let it out louder than she'd meant to.

Lucy looked at her. "I always have a saltine after a pill," she said. "Helps my stomach." Which she rubbed.

Angelina glanced at the glass still in Lucy's hand.

"From last night," she said. "I always try to leave a little Ernst and Julio in the glass. Something to look forward to the next day."

Angelina wondered why she'd never thought of that.

Back at the table, she glanced at her watch. "Wow. It's already time for me to go." HomeHealthCare had a two-hour limit.

"What about all the bottles?" Lucy asked, still standing.

"I'll be back on Thursday." Angelina gathered her papers and put the scale back in her tote. "And I can help you change the light bulb over the sink."

"John Milton said he'd get some bulbs."

"Was that...?"

Keeping both hands on the walker, Lucy nodded, tipping her head toward the back, which Angelina took to mean the peeing. "Course he's been saying he'd do it ever since the summer."

"I bet I can find an extra bulb at home," Angelina said.

When she opened the door, Lady barked, sounding as if she were right behind her. Angelina lunged to the cement block and hurried to her car, holding tight to her closed blue umbrella.

CHAPTER 6

Will knew Angelina didn't have to go to work this morning, so he removed two of the colorful, thin-striped placemats from the drawer and arranged them on the table with the fringed edges touching. He added matching napkins and silverware and stepped back to make sure he hadn't forgotten anything.

A door closed upstairs, then Angelina's light steps. He looked toward the hall. "Angelina?"

When she came into view, she was wearing black warm-up pants and a white V-necked shirt.

"Do you want juice?" he asked.

She shook her head. As she turned to the desk, he noticed how the back of her hair fell long and straight. No fuss. Her face either. He knew without having noticed that she wore no lipstick. She never had. She was still the same Angelina he'd fallen in love with so long ago. And then some, he was reminded as she turned around—her breasts had filled out over the years. In her hands were her keys.

"Is scrambled okay?"

"I'm going to the gym," she said.

"Since when?"

"Since today. That one near here." Then she dropped a tea bag into the Starbucks mug she used for the car, added hot water, gave him a quick kiss on the lips, and closed the door behind her.

Will collapsed into his place at the table. He should be glad she was going out. There was a time he'd thought that her mother's agoraphobia also pulsed through her genes and that she'd never leave the house again. He stood to look through the back windows at their porch. He could still see Angelina in that yellow maternity top—very pregnant with Cara—putting two yellow placemats on the new wrought iron table.

It had been early summer, a cool morning, right after they'd moved into the house, one of the first ones to be built in the neighborhood, and Angelina wanted to have breakfast outside. He was making another pot of coffee when she headed to the patio with a bowl of cantaloupe and a basket of her blueberry muffins—the first thing she'd ever made for him. After that morning, she never made them again.

When he heard her screams, a snake was his first thought; that she'd fallen, his second. His body moved in slow motion as he tried to reach her, seeing the enormous blackbirds through the windows—one on her head, one at her feet, two strutting around the table.

"Angelina," he'd shouted over her yelling and the birds' screeching. "I'm here." But he was only just opening the patio door, had not yet reached her. He had nightmares even now in which he never did.

In front of him, she was huddled over, crying out, protecting her face with her hand and her stomach with the basket of muffins. The cantaloupe lay helter-skelter on the table.

"Throw the muffins," he shouted as he was finally close enough to strike at the iridescent birds with their freakishly long tails. He tried to wrestle the basket away, but she wouldn't let go. He gave up on the basket and grabbed the warm muffins—shielding her with his other arm—throwing them as far as he could into the woods. He swept the cantaloupe off the table and kicked it off the patio. The birds followed, and he cradled her in his arms and carried her into the house. On the sofa, he rocked her back and forth, telling her over and over again that she was safe, that she was okay, that he would never let that happen again. When she calmed down, he cleaned the small wounds on her arm and head and called the doctor. Because she was pregnant, they would treat the bites with antibiotic cream unless they became infected.

She would not go outside, would not leave the house.

After a few days, Will encouraged her to return to work, but she quit her job at the hospital, saying the baby would be here soon anyway.

Why in the world had it been birds? It was as if she were nine years old again, afraid to open the door.

And they had both looked so forward to the patio.

The next weekend, Will began to screen it in, hammering out his frustrations, trying to cover up the sound of all the birds in all the world. But it had been the baby who saved her—who saved them—the baby who had broken the spell. They could look at Cara instead of scanning for birds.

Cara was also the one who managed to get Angelina back on the porch. Will was out there with her when she took her first steps, and he called Angelina to come see. She stepped right out the door as if nothing had ever happened.

He never told her, but he'd called animal control to report the incident. The woman on the phone suspected grackles by the purple underbelly, yellow eyes, and the high-pitched screeching. "Like a rusty gate," was how Will had described it. Other incidents had been reported, she'd said. Two others nearby. It was baby bird season, the woman had explained, the birds on the offensive to feed and protect their fledglings.

Will's stomach growled, and he stood and zapped the bacon for another minute. Without Angelina, he could eat all four pieces. And he could read the paper. On the front stoop, before bending to retrieve it, he arched his back and took a moment to survey, through the drizzle, the three box-like houses on the other side of the street. He wasn't sure he'd ever noticed how similar they were. Back at the stove, he swallowed coffee and cracked two eggs into the skillet. He replaced her egg in the refrigerator; her placemat, silverware, and napkin in their drawers. Then he waited at the stove, holding the spatula, ready as soon as the eggs were.

Eggs onto the plate, bacon lined up next to the eggs, grease into the coffee tin. Will carried his plate to the table. This spread sure beat a banana while driving to work, but he should have made toast. He'd get the hang of it after a day or two.

When the doorbell rang, he was drinking his third cup of coffee and still working on the paper. He looked toward the front of the house. Who in the world could that be?

"I was beginning to think nobody was home," the man said, brushing by him. He was taller than Will, in some sort of uniformed shirt, and carrying a metal canister. Will glanced out at the truck and saw Spratlin Pest Control in large red letters on the side.

"You minding the fort? Where's Mrs. Brooks?" He set the canister down and unhooked a long, silver nozzle.

"Exercise."

"Rick," the man said, wiping his hand on his pants and then extending it.

"Will," he said, reluctantly shaking Rick's hand. Rick had a strong grip and looked as if he might lift weights. His name was stitched in red on a pale-yellow shirt with short sleeves barely wide enough for his biceps. Will felt his stomach pushing against his belt. He stood up straighter.

"I like to exercise too," Rick said, picking up the canister and heading into the dining room, spraying along the edge of the floors as he glided through the room and into the kitchen.

Will followed him and scooped his plate and glass off the table. By the time he turned the water on the already-dried egg remains and orange pulp, Rick's voice was coming from the den.

"Yeah," Rick said. "Normally I come on Tuesday, but the Mrs. cancelled on me a couple of weeks ago. Today's the first time I could work her back in. We've been some kind of busy the last few weeks."

When Will went into the den, Rick was already slipping into the hall, squirting here and there as he turned to the stairs. Will wondered if Angelina went upstairs with him, then he felt ridiculous and uneasy at the same time. He cleared his throat. He had no idea if he was supposed to stay with Rick or not, but Rick wasn't waiting for him, and he seemed to know where he was going. So Will just stood there in the den—hoping that's what Angelina did—and about five minutes later, Rick came down the steps whistling. Then, without stopping, he swung around the stairs, opened the door to the basement, and headed down those steps.

Back in the kitchen, Will filed his placemat away, wiped the crumbs into his hand, and brushed them off into the trash, thinking the whole time the odd thought that Rick seemed more comfortable in this house than he did. In the den, he dropped the newspaper onto his chair and waited with his hands in his pockets.

When Rick clomped back into view and set the canister down, he extracted a piece of paper from his breast pocket, which he handed to Will. "So you got you a day off today, huh? I'd like a day off too, but that's not likely to happen. You gotta love pest control in the South. Never a dull moment."

Will inched toward the front door, then opened it.

Rick followed him, putting his canister down again next to the umbrella stand. "Do you need a pen?" he asked, pointing one at Will.

Will, now seeing the X, took the pen and signed the receipt. Rick waved behind him as he headed down the cobblestones. "All this rain is something, isn't it? Tell the Mrs. I'll be back to the regular schedule next month."

Will left their copy on the narrow table by the front door and went into the dining room. In front of the windows, he watched Rick back out of the drive. Not quite nine thirty. He rubbed his palms together as if anticipating a meal laid out before him, but he was thinking *now what?* He was tired of having a plan, yet every bone in his body craved one.

In front of the windows, jiggling the change in his pocket, he looked around, wishing for Angelina. And then he remembered the basement. At the bottom of the steps, it smelled a little musty, but mostly Will noticed the chemical smell from the pesticide. He opened the door to the playroom, but when he parted the curtains, he saw that trees blocked a good deal of the light. He closed the door back and crossed the hall to the guest room that he couldn't remember anyone ever staying in. As he pulled the curtains open, light flooded the space. *This would work. It sure would.* He turned to face the room, what little of it there was since Angelina had the bed in the middle. He would ask her if he could push it up into the corner and if he could take down these curtains.

Hell, Rick wouldn't ask Angelina. He would just clomp down those steps and push the bed up against the wall. Well, this was his house too, wasn't it? If Rick wouldn't ask, then neither would he.

Was that the doorbell again? He would never get anything done if he had to keep answering the door. Will clomped up the stairs and opened it.

The FedEx man's smile disappeared, and he slid the photos he was holding into his shirt pocket stitched with *Dale*. "How are you today, sir? I just need a signature."

Will signed some sort of electronic thing that reminded him of the Etch-A-Sketch the girls used to have, then Dale gave him a package and told him to have a nice day. Will managed a "you too" and shut the door. He tossed the package, which was from Livie's study-abroad program, on top of the pest control receipt. At least Dale hadn't come inside the house.

CHAPTER 7

Inside the gym, Angelina stepped onto one of twelve treadmills that faced six flat-screen TVs that hung from the ceiling. In front of her, a small woman with a neat little ponytail bounced by. And behind her came two plain-looking people, dressed in washed-out colors and stretched-out shirts, holding hands. The man had pulled his dark socks high on his calves. And the woman he was pulling along behind him had on navy Keds.

Angelina checked her phone. No messages. Usually by this time of day she had something from one of the girls. And something from Kate. She had so much to tell Kate, but Kate was volunteering at a women's legal center in South Africa until the new year.

A lifetime ago, when she and Kate shared an apartment, Angelina had loved nursing as much as Kate loved the law. They were always vying with each other for who was doing the most good in the world, Kate winning over and over again, and still. Of course, that was only half the conversation. The other half was the next date. Angelina was handicapped in that regard since North Georgia Hospital had started her with the graveyard shift, but it turned out she would rather be at the hospital in the middle of the night, with its quiet halls and lack of chatter, than win in the love category, even though she won anyway, and still.

Years ago, after being married only three months, Kate had filed for divorce. Marriage, she'd said, the very idea of it, was flawed. Kate did not say this only one time; she said it at every opportunity. She'd said it again the last time they had lunch—right before she'd flown to Cape Town and before Angelina and Will had taken Iris to school. They'd met in Atlanta, near Kate's office in Buckhead, at some little diner because Kate wanted breakfast and Angelina didn't care.

"I never have time to eat breakfast," Kate had said. "And it's my favorite meal."

"You and Will should hang out together," Angelina said.

"How is Will?"

"The same." And they laughed, like they always did.

"So," Kate had said, "another one bites the dust. You know my friends the Thompsons? High school sweethearts. And after twenty years of marriage, they can't stand each other. That's what marriage does to love."

Angelina took a bite of her scrambled egg sandwich.

"Number one, all that compromising is bad for a person."

Angelina picked up her mug of tea and sat back to let Kate do her thing.

"Number two, forever is ridiculous. People change. I should become a politician and sponsor a bill to do away with marriage. 'Protect love. Ban marriage.' I'd put it on t-shirts, mugs, and bumper stickers."

"How's Mike?" Angelina asked, grinning.

"He's great," Kate said. "Except he mentioned moving in together again. High mortgage payments were his excuse this time. I don't think he's serious. He knows I'll never sell, or share, my place. He'll cool off while I'm gone."

"You know, Will is not the problem."

"I know, sweetie."

"He's just kind of in my way and keeping me from getting to the real problem. But after next week when we take Iris to Ole Miss, that won't matter. I'll have all that time and space. I can finally get back to being me—whoever that might be at this point."

Angelina looked down. She'd only been on the treadmill twelve minutes. At least Kate would be happy she was out of the house.

The plain couple was bouncing her way again, no longer holding hands but bumping shoulders and elbows as if they had to be connected somehow. Angelina felt her face getting red and her mouth, dry. The woman mounted a treadmill on the row in front of Angelina, as did the man, right beside his companion. Angelina wondered what their names were. Nadine came immediately to mind. She struggled a few minutes before she came up with Francis for him. Well, Nadine and Francis were perfect for each other—his socks and her Keds.

Judgmental, that's what *her* name should be. She raised her eyes to the six screens—a cooking show, fighting in Afghanistan, a woman dancing with a microphone whose movements seemed to be loosely connected to the blaring music, a weather report showing a map of the United States, again the woman dancing, and finally a plea from the Red Cross. Angelina tried to breathe evenly—in as much as out—and she felt the color leave her face, her heart rate slow. It felt good to tip her head up, to rest her eyes on something in the distance.

CHAPTER 8

Getting to the porch, this thing he and Angelina used to do right after he got home from work, had been a struggle again tonight. When he'd suggested it around five thirty, her response had been "Now?" He'd shrugged. While she called Cara back, he took a laundry basket upstairs. When he returned with his dirty clothes, she went upstairs.

But they were here now. The low plywood skirting and copper screen as tight as when he'd added them years ago. He pressed on the screen again—no give at all.

Angelina rocked as she told him about her visit with Lucy the day before. "She's—I don't know—she's different."

"She sounds gross—maggots and knives and the smell. And so fat."

"But she's not gross. I can't explain it. She's not."

"And you're only going to have one patient at a time?" Will asked.

"Yes," she said, her voice far away. "Part-time work. One patient."

He went closer, sitting beside her, tightening his grip on his glass as if it were in danger of slipping out of his grasp.

"That's the way I want to do it," she said. "And they're desperate for nurses. Home care nurses." She looked at Will. "Apparently, everybody wants to stay at home." She took a sip of wine. "I think they hope I'll eventually be full-time."

"Is that what you want?" he asked, the words sounding weak even to him.

"I don't know what I want," she said.

"Makes sense they need nurses. Your father always said you could count on people to get sick and to get old."

"Only he got neither," she said, placing her empty glass on the table as if that were that.

Now he looked away, but into the darkened house, only a faint light on here and there. Earlier this evening, when she'd finally come back downstairs, she'd gone straight into the kitchen. From his chair in the den, he heard the light clanks of wine glasses on the counter and then the suction release of the refrigerator door. He'd smiled to himself. He wanted to tell her about his day, how he'd moved the bed up against the wall and found a card table in the attic he could use as a temporary worktable, how he'd also brought down their old table to refinish for Cara, how he'd gone to the hardware store for a new sander and supplies, how he was working on a key rack for the back door. How he had a work-room. But when he'd ventured into the kitchen, his glass sat on the counter, empty.

Years ago, after Livie was born, he'd noticed that when he came in from the Water Works and said hello, Angelina would answer without looking at him while she continued doing what-ever she was doing—chopping a carrot, heating a bottle, stirring soup, setting the table, folding laundry. Cara would be every-where, pots and pans on the floor, and Livie in the swing. He would stand in the kitchen and go through the mail. When he would ask how her day was, "fine" is all she would say.

One evening, she'd told him, "When you come home, your day is over. You can relax. Life is easy. But my day is still going. My day never ends."

Instead of pointing out all the things he did—load the dishwasher, help with baths, read to the girls—he'd suggested that when he got home, they sit together on the porch. After that, they used his arrival as a rest stop for her, a coming together for them, a joining of forces. They would shut the door on things that needed to be done—on supper and the girls, keeping an eye on them through the window when they were little, ignoring them when they were older.

He and Angelina arrived on the porch as two separate beings and went back inside as one. And that's all he wanted now—to be connected. To *stay* connected. He knew if he could wait, she would come to him.

For now, however, neither *he* nor the porch was working. He looked in the direction she was looking, but all he could see was darkness.

CHAPTER 9

On her second visit to Lucy, as Angelina pulled up in front of trailer #1, she wondered who lived in the other two. There were no cars, so whoever the people were, they must work. Again, Angelina stood on the cement block in front of the beat-up aluminum door. This time, along with the barking, she heard Lucy say, "She's tied up already." And when the door opened, Lucy added, "Oh, I meant to put out the Halloween decorations before you got here."

Inside, something definitely smelled bad.

Lucy, in the same faded housedress she'd worn on the previous visit, hobbled toward the chest of drawers.

"No walker?"

"Nothing but a nuisance." Lucy opened the top drawer, then cried out, putting her fingers on her nose.

Angelina smelled something worse, an intensely rotten smell.

"All the decorations are ruined," Lucy said, still holding her nose.

Angelina backed to the door, keeping her eyes on Lucy, who pulled the whole drawer out.

"Lucy, be careful."

"Damned maggots," Lucy said. "John Milton must have put that little pumpkin in here last year. Now it's ruined the witch, the turkey, and the Santa Claus I gave him." And she started toward Angelina with the drawer out in front of her.

"I believe you," Angelina said.

Lucy rolled her eyes. "You're blocking the door," she said. "How about opening it?"

Which Angelina did, and then she stared as Lucy dropped the entire drawer outside, wiped her hands together and then on her housedress. As if to herself, she said, "John Milton can deal with that later."

They sat at the card table, and while Angelina finished organizing Lucy's meds, putting the families of bottles in the small Ziploc bags she'd brought, Lucy snacked on candy corn from a ripped-open bag on the table.

"So John Milton's a sign painter?"

"In the sky," Lucy said. "His first day of school, that's when it all started. He got home, and he couldn't open his spelling book fast enough. Inside were these signs he'd made on that creamy paper with the thin red and blue lines. He'd folded them to fit inside the book. 'To protect them,' he'd said, his face flushed and his long black curls matted around the edges. When I went out to work that night, I stopped by the convenience store and bought one pack of eight crayons and one pack of index cards. At home, I counted out eight cards and put them by his place at the table next to those brand-new crayons. Ever since, he's always carried crayons and cards with him. I never let him run out. *Lemonade five cents.* Yellow stand with blue writing. *Fourth grade play: The Wizard of Oz.* He used all eight colors on that one. *Seventh Grade Play: Anne Frank.* Only black and white. *Sign Painter: $1/a sign.* All colors. *Senior Play: Lil' Abner.* Lots of red."

Angelina leaned back in her chair, tipping the front legs off the ground.

"I pushed him," Lucy said. "Bigger, better. That's the way the world works, I told him. And I bought bigger and bigger packs of crayons until I got to that box of a hundred and twenty. You know, the one with the two levels and a sharpener?"

It had been years since Angelina had thought about crayons.

"He picked up twenty-three reds in one little fist and nineteen blues in the other. He'd counted them. 'Too much,' he said. 'One red and one blue is all I want.'"

After she took Lucy's blood pressure, which was still high, Angelina said, "Lucy, we need to talk about your weight."

"How about one of my other problems?"

Angelina took off her black sweater, letting it fold over the back of the chair. She leaned forward onto the table, opened her hands, and said, tapping her right pointer finger on each finger of her left hand as she counted off the benefits, "Losing weight would improve your diabetes, your high blood pressure, and your high cholesterol. It would be good for your heart. You would feel better."

Lucy pushed another piece of candy corn into her mouth.

"Don't you want to be your best self?"

Lucy's eyes cut to Angelina. "There's only one me," Lucy said. "This is it."

Angelina wondered if Lucy truly felt no conflict between the way she was and the way she wanted to be.

"There's no skinny person inside me waiting to get out," Lucy said.

"What I meant—"

"I'm hungry all the time."

"What are you hungry for?" Angelina asked.

"Something salty." Lucy shifted her weight in the chair and scratched at a scab on her elbow.

Angelina looked toward the kitchen. "Like…"

"Then something sweet," Lucy said, her fingers acting like little mice climbing through the hole in the plastic of the candy corn bag.

"Lucy, I'm serious."

"It's a vicious circle," Lucy said.

"Are you hungry right now?"

"I'm always hungry."

"Right now?"

"I think so," Lucy said. "Yes."

"You don't *think* hunger. You *feel* it."

Lucy put her hand on her stomach as if she were reading a crystal ball. "Yes. I'm hungry."

"What do you want to eat?"

"Right now?"

"Yes."

"A chocolate-glazed, cream-filled donut. Gracie probably has some over at the 7-Eleven."

"That's not hunger."

"See, I can't trust myself," Lucy said in a voice that just as easily could have been saying *I'll match your bet and raise you five.*

"Jeez, Lucy. There's more to life than food."

CHAPTER 10

After leaving Lucy's, Angelina drove straight home, but when she saw the garage door up and Will's car inside, she kept going. The empty house of her dreams had always included Will in the morning and evening, but now, since he was there all the time, it excluded him.

A beat-up silver car passed her with a bumper sticker on the rear windshield that read, in purple letters, "I'm a what-if kind of girl." Angelina wanted to know what that kind of girl looked like. She sped up but couldn't get into the other lane, and the silver car bolted through the yellow light for which Angelina stopped.

The sky was no longer as clear as it had been that morning. Now there were layers of clouds—white, gray, bluish white. The gray layer was thinner than the others, and the clouds all seemed stuck on to the sky, as if they might stay that way and never progress to clear or rain.

Moving again, she followed the line of cars. The first time she'd ever seen Will, he was leaning against the balcony of the hospitality suite in the Savannah hotel where she was staying for a friend's wedding, his button-down white shirt sleeves rolled up to just below his elbows, a beer in his hand, and those eyes. He was the man with whom she had built a life. They had been on the same track, both wanting the same things. But Will had driven his last car until the bumper fell off.

67

Angelina needed air. She turned into an office parking lot and threw open the door. She breathed in, then stood, and leaned against the hard body of the car. Her stomach growled, and she imagined Will standing in their kitchen waiting for her, a colorful placemat in each hand.

Across the parking lot, inside the office building, a man was standing at the window. Was he wondering where his wife was? Or was he thinking he didn't want to go home? He wasn't beating on the glass like Ben at the end of *The Graduate*, at the top of the church. She wasn't Elaine about to run away from her own wedding. Angelina remembered the last scene, when they were on the bus, their faces staring straight ahead, their eyes so wide. What now, but also, what if?

A woman came into the man's office, and he turned away. Angelina reached into her pockets while kicking at several acorns on the ground, but her pockets were empty. No gloves or ChapStick or tissue. Her fingers moved freely in the soft emptiness. What if she didn't do what she was supposed to?

She turned around and leaned the front of her body against the car, resting her chin in her hands on the roof. She could see the Blue Ridge Mountains that for some scientific reason looked more blue than green. They began here in Georgia, then rippled through South Carolina, North Carolina, Tennessee, Virginia, West Virginia, Maryland, and finally stopped somewhere in Pennsylvania.

CHAPTER 11

Angelina opened her eyes in the dark. When she felt Will start to roll, she clutched the sheets, felt them pull taut, and then jerked them back to her side. When she used to let Will pull the covers an inch every time he rolled over, by morning she was completely uncovered. Now she slept holding on. Besides, it would take a lot more than yanking the sheets to wake Will. He'd never heard the girls crying when they were babies.

4:02 a.m. Only three in Mississippi. She wondered if Iris were still awake. It was already ten in Paris. Livie would be in class. Cara was surely sleeping soundly. She always had. Angelina wondered if Lucy were asleep or lying in the dark awake. She got up. *Don't think.* She looked out the windows and noticed it was lighter than black. She should get the oil changed in her car tomorrow after she got through at the office. She knocked into the door molding, sending herself at a diagonal into the bathroom, right on track for the toilet. *Don't think.* If she did, she'd be up for hours. *Flush. Don't think.* It was too late to take a Xanax. *Aim for the bed.*

She nestled back onto her side in her little spot of bed—a pillow to her back and another to her chest. She weighted her eyes shut with a rectangular silk bean bag. Wide awake. All those years that the girls would wake her in the middle of the night—first as babies, then with bad dreams, and then coming in after dates. Now she could finally sleep through the night again, only she couldn't. She slipped out of bed and out of their room into the hall. Not only had she never been able to see over one stage to the next, she'd never thought to look behind her either. Now she leaned against the wall to stare at the line of closed doors, no music or light seeping out from under the bottoms. Just darkness, accompanied by the sound of a dripping faucet from one of the bathrooms.

CHAPTER 12

In the bedroom, Angelina covered her head with a pillow, but she could still hear the drawer opening, the plunk of the coffee can, the running water, the click of the lid. In a minute, she'd smell coffee. Will continued to get up before she did, just as he had when he was working, but these days he set about making breakfast—lavish breakfasts. The smells of eggs and sausage—and bacon—lingering in the house the entire day.

Twenty minutes later, she breezed into the kitchen.

Will, standing by the stove, looked up, half an eggshell in each hand, two placemats on the table.

She scooped up her purse and keys.

"Don't you want some?" he asked.

"I'll grab some coffee at work."

"When will you be back?"

"Not sure," she said lightly, as if nothing stood behind his question or her answer. "I might go to the gym after the meeting." She kissed his cheek and spun herself out the door.

At the end of the driveway, she paused as a car went by, and she remembered how she used to care about placemats. And matching napkins and tears in the wallpaper and cracks in the plaster. Now she backed out, looking at the house as she did these days, from the street as she drove past, and seeing Will with his mouth open—needing, needing, needing.

She banged her fist on the steering wheel. Will was a good person; she was the awful one. And she was getting distracted—farther and farther away from why she had wanted the empty house in the first place. She felt as wound up as a top, as if a giant's finger were holding her in place until he could get far enough away to be out of danger when he let go.

After the short Friday meeting at HomeHealthCare, Angelina did go to the gym. On the treadmill, to the sound of very loud rap music, she scanned the room in front of her. A woman wearing makeup in a red t-shirt with the word TRAINER across the front was leading two college-aged girls—each one in a shirt that matched her shorts—toward the machines in front of the windows. And there were Nadine and Francis. Angelina almost waved. Nadine wore old-fashioned glasses in black frames, and Angelina saw now that she had buck teeth. While Nadine was preparing to use a machine, Francis, in his dark socks, sat across from her—not exercising, just watching. His eyes followed her body as she moved from adjusting the weight to adjusting the seat. Then he watched her lift with her legs as if she were levitating a person. As she finished, he crossed the tiny space that separated them and stood too close to her. With a white towel, he gently dotted the sweat from her forehead and from each cheek. Then he paused before kissing her on the mouth. Right there, in the gym, amidst the loud music, the sweat, and the people lifting and squatting.

Angelina looked around to see if anyone else had noticed, but Nadine and Francis seemed to be her own private reality show. Next would be a close-up of Nadine talking to the camera. *What do I do when I'm feeling wild and crazy? I go down to the 7-Eleven and buy one of those tall beers and a pack of cigarettes. It doesn't get any better than that. A favorite magazine? Never look at them.* And then the camera would zoom into the Keds and the too-short pants and the bobby pins that held the strands that wouldn't stay in the ponytail. A style she should under no circumstances have put her boring, brown hair in, after parting it in the middle so that these wings hung down from each side, not because they'd escaped from the pins but because she'd singled them out to hang as wings.

Angelina's face heated up. She was hateful, and she reached for her throat. Judging others was as automatic as breathing, and she wanted it to stop. She wanted her first response to be open arms.

Nadine and Francis were ambling toward the treadmills. He had a finger on her back, which seemed to be making her smile. And not just smile. Nadine was glowing. In her bobby pins and Keds, she sparkled. As if she were happy just the way she was.

Angelina's cell phone beeped. *Out of milk.* She put it back in the little phone slot on the treadmill and increased both the speed and the incline, then she set her eyes on the six screens above her.

CHAPTER 13

Instead of the jingle that accompanied so many door openings, Will heard "I Am a Patriot" in Jackson Browne's unmistakable voice as he entered the new coffee shop he'd noticed a few weeks ago when he used to go to work. He laughed out loud. Music—he'd forgotten about music.

And he would have gone straight back out the door to set up some sort of music situation in his workroom if a tall guy had not popped up behind the counter, slinging his long, straight hair out of his eyes and saying, "Hi, my name is Clyde. What can I get ya?"

Will nodded and stepped forward, staring at the chalkboard above the shelves of mugs and Mason jars of coffee beans. He was pretty sure he was going to order a cappuccino because that was something he couldn't make at home. Under a dome on a cake stand sitting on the counter were sugar-sprinkled cranberry muffins that looked really good. Too bad he was between meals.

After he ordered, Clyde said, "For here or to go?"

"Here," Will said, "for god's sake." He felt like he hadn't been out of the house in years.

"Cool," Clyde said.

There was no one else there.

Will wished he'd grabbed his book. Mental note for next time. "So, Clyde, do you have a girlfriend?"

Clyde stopped blasting the milk. "A girlfriend? Yep, I do." More blasting.

"Does she like being around you?" Will leaned his hip against the counter.

Again, Clyde stopped blasting. "Isn't that kinda the point of a girlfriend?"

"Fair enough," Will said, inhaling that rich coffee smell. "And good for you."

Clyde loomed over the cappuccino machine, frowning as he slowly transferred the mug with precipitous foam to the wooden counter and then began to slide it across. As soon as the mug made it halfway, Clyde let go and again slung his long bangs out of his eyes.

Will put down a five and rotated the mug so he could hold the handle. The wording on the side was "Running on Empty?" He laughed again, thinking Angelina would love this place.

"My mother's crazy for Jackson Browne," Clyde said, rolling his eyes.

Will dropped the change into the Mason jar on the counter. "So what do you do when you want a girl to like you?" he asked, tipping his head to drink some of the coffee but getting only foam.

"I don't think I do anything particular," Clyde said.

"Guess how long I've been married."

Clyde shrugged.

"Come on, take a guess."

"Nine years," Clyde said.

"Twenty-three."

"Man, the whole time I've been alive. I'm thinking ten years is a good amount of time to shoot for."

"My father left my mother after ten years," Will said, and then he paused, hearing music. Had it been playing the whole time? He located tiny rectangular speakers in the ceiling at the corners of the room. "I never spoke to him again."

"That's harsh, man."

"And my wife's mother was crazy," he said, leaning against the counter. "Never left the house. Died in her bathtub, where she'd been for days. You want to know the ironic thing?"

Clyde nodded almost imperceptibly.

"My wife doesn't want to be in the house at all." He took a gulp of coffee and again came away with nothing but foam. "You really have to drink down in this to get the coffee, don't you?"

"I don't drink cappuccino."

"Maybe I shouldn't drink cappuccino." But he did get some coffee on his next try. "Hell, I was afraid of the wrong thing."

"We have a patio out back if you'd like to sit outside," Clyde said.

Will thought he would.

"Under the Falling Sky" was playing on the patio too, and Will followed the sound over his shoulder to the small black speaker above the door. The patio was a new-looking cement square at the rear of the restaurant, away from the road. Three picnic tables. To the right was a large sprawling oak, the leaves at the top an intense red. Heading to a table, Will crunched over a sprinkling of brown leaves, which he suspected Clyde was supposed to have swept up. He sat, and after taking a swig of coffee, he wiped the foam above his lip with the back of his hand. By the last few notes of "Looking Into You," Will remembered

"Rock Me On the Water" would be next. These were Angelina's songs—songs he knew from listening with her.

Some kind of brown bird landed on the edge of the picnic table, then hopped closer, its tail feathers sticking up in the air. He picked up a stick, but before he could poke at the bird, it flew away.

CHAPTER 14

Angelina eased in beside a bright and shiny red truck parked in front of trailer #1 just as the door to Lucy's trailer opened and out came the big bear, staring as if he could see through her. Usually when a man did that, it made her nervous and she looked away. But there was something about John Milton's face that she couldn't look away from. She turned off the car.

His black hair still stuck out from his head and from his arms, and his t-shirt still didn't quite cover his stomach that for some odd—very odd—reason she wanted to touch. The t-shirt was wrinkled. He probably rolled out of bed and picked up the first thing he saw on the ground. And he probably slept naked. Not probably. Of course he did.

Which made her face hot and caused her to be aware that she was still sitting in the truck. *Just* sitting here. She busied herself collecting her things—the light bulb she'd finally remembered that she stuffed into her shoulder bag, the stepladder, and the sky-blue umbrella from the floor.

As she opened her car door, the red truck rumbled off, John Milton not looking back as he accelerated toward the road.

Good, she thought, he was gone, and yet she felt a draining away. She'd been bracing for some sort of confrontation—something to do with the way he looked at her, the way his look challenged her. But to what she wasn't sure.

The drawer of decorations and maggots was gone. Angelina knocked. At the sound of the barking, she heard Lucy say, "She's tied up. She's tied up."

Lucy did not wait to greet her but rocked from one foot to the other toward her chair.

Angelina clunked in, dropped her purse on a chair, noticed the drawer in fact back in the chest, the pill bottles still grouped in Ziploc bags in the purple bucket on the middle of the card table, and the same sickly-sweet smell as before. While she was unfolding the stepladder, out of the corner of her eye she saw another maggot clinging to the drain. She'd been hoping that cleaning out the drawer would be the end of the maggots. Surely John Milton *did* clean out the drawer.

Because the light fixture lined up over the sink, Angelina couldn't get the ladder directly underneath it, and she had to reach forward to undo the four screws. Now she smelled somthing more like cabbage or liver, and she looked toward the stove but nothing was cooking. The fixture inched a little to the side and small dusty particles trickled out. She closed her eyes and turned her head away.

"Damn," Lucy said, now standing.

"What?"

"Maggots."

"Yeah, I saw the one in the sink," Angelina said. "I thought we'd take care of him after I change the light." She almost had it undone, and it suddenly felt heavy.

"No," Lucy said. "Now there are..."

And then something large fell out of the opening she'd created in the ceiling, and they both screamed. Angelina jumped off the ladder, holding a fixture that was crawling with squirmy maggots—too many to count. She ran to the door, opened it, sent them and the fixture flying, then closed the door, leaning against it as if the maggots might try to get back in.

"God help us," she heard Lucy saying, over and over again, as she stared at the sink with both hands over her nose.

Angelina covered her own nose with her arm and stepped closer. Maggots—hundreds of them—and flies and the bushy tail of a squirrel. Before she could make it outside, she threw up, only having time to pull out the front of her sweater as a receptacle, and as she reached for the knob, she heard Lucy right behind her.

Hugging the trailer, Angelina tried to stay under the too-small protective overhang on the opposite side from where the light fixture had landed. She reached behind her, wadding her sweater up in her hand, then bringing the back over the front and getting it off. She looked for a place to put it and then just tossed it away from the trailer. She wanted a Coke. When she was a child, her mother always brought her a Coke after she threw up.

She leaned her head back against the trailer and closed her eyes, but the dead squirrel was falling from the ceiling *on her*. With her eyes open, she saw a murder of crows on the telephone line close to the road.

Anyway, she couldn't leave. Her keys were in her purse, which was inside with the dead squirrel and the maggots.

Which reminded her of Lucy. Who had her hand on her heart and no color. Angelina stepped closer and reached for Lucy's wrist to check her pulse, which was rapid but steady. She helped Lucy into a folding chair, its plastic madras ribbons unraveling around the edges.

"Breathe with me slowly. Now cough."

Dainty was a word Angelina would never want applied to herself and never would have thought could be applied to Lucy. But Lucy's cough was dainty. "Cough harder, Lucy."

"I don't need to cough."

"Coughing squeezes the heart. Puts pressure on it. Helps it regain its normal rhythm."

"You're telling me that putting pressure on my heart is a good thing?"

"Do you have any pain?"

"I used to be able to move that fast no problem."

How could Lucy not have noticed maggots falling from the ceiling?

"There was a squirrel up there," Lucy said, flicking a long piece of grass back and forth with her foot.

"Why didn't you ask John Milton to help you find the maggots?"

"Do you have children?"

"Someone's got to clean this up."

Lucy looked at her.

"I'm a nurse, Lucy."

When Lucy turned to the street, Angelina sat down on the other side of the door on a large, rusted paint drum. While Lucy watched the street, Angelina watched the crows. Without her sweater, she was chilly. Lucy wore a short gray one, but it hardly covered her. Angelina turned back to the crows. And there they sat on each side of the door.

Lucy patted herself, then reached into a pocket and pulled out a movie-sized box of Hot Tamales. She poured a handful for herself and, keeping her eyes on the street, passed the box across the small cinder-block space that separated them toward Angelina, who took the box, poured a handful of red candy for herself, and passed them back. When she did, she saw something about Lucy that reminded her of Nadine. Lucy kind of sparkled or glowed. She looked content.

In the true-blue sky, the white clouds floated a little more freely than usual, as if someone might be in the process of cutting them loose.

After a while, Angelina stood up. "Lucy, we've got a mess in there."

"I know it," Lucy said.

"And my purse and keys are in there, so I've got to go back in. And your life is in there, so you do too."

Lucy looked at her. Her lips parted. Angelina imagined her saying, *To hell with it, let's just walk away.*

"The longer we wait," Angelina said, "the farther away the maggots can get. What do we have to work with?"

"I think there're some Walmart bags in the closet on the right."

Angelina extended her hand to Lucy, who took it. Angelina stepped back for Lucy to go in first.

Inside, they stayed close to the exterior wall and close together. Lucy opened the hall closet and passed Angelina two large gray-blue Walmart bags stuffed full of other Walmart bags.

"Any cleaning supplies in there? Or gloves?" Angelina was not breathing through her nose.

Lucy looked and shook her head.

"Okay, first thing is to get that mess out of here." As if they were two kids, pulling items from a dress-up trunk, Angelina said, "I'm going to take three of these really big bags and put them one inside the other. Here, take these two smaller bags and put them over your hands, like gloves."

Lucy took the bags and started covering her hands.

"Once we have the squirrel in the bag," Angelina said, "what are we going to do with it?"

"There's a dumpster over at the 7-Eleven." Lucy nodded to the left.

"So you can take it over there."

"You could drive it over there."

"Lucy, the dead squirrel is not going in my car."

"Do you think I should walk that far?"

"You're supposed to be walking that far every day," Angelina said, placing a bag on each of her hands. "We talked about that last time, right before I left."

"Except I haven't."

Angelina sighed.

"I'll stay here and catch maggots," Lucy said. "That'll be my part."

"Let's try not to think about it. We'll each pick up an end of the squirrel. We'll get it in the bag. I'll knot up the end and head to the dumpster."

Lucy held up her Walmarted hands.

In spite of herself, Angelina held up hers in response.

And then, their bagged hands raised like guns, they emerged from the hallway. Angelina had some hope the dead squirrel would not still be there. Of course it was. Plus flies.

Blue plastic hands reaching in, picking up an end, but coming away with only a small piece of squirrel. Angelina gagged. Without speaking, they reached down again for more. *Look at the crinkly plastic bag. Look at the letters that spell Walmart.* She and Lucy, piece by piece, managed to get the squirrel and most of the gelatinous maggots and flies inside the large bag. Angelina twirled the bag around and then knotted it.

Before she shut the door, Angelina glanced back at Lucy, who had an open bag in one hand and a fork in the other.

CHAPTER 15

What had been a clear blue day had changed into a cloudy evening, moist particles of air floating through the porch screen. The bright, vibrant reds and golds that had finally arrived appeared muted through the surrounding grayness, reminding Angelina, even before the colors had reached their peak, how much she looked forward to watching the trees shake off the dead leaves. She zipped her porch jacket halfway up over the clean t-shirt and the p.j. bottoms she'd put on after her bath, resting the palm of her hand on the soft, weathered gray material of Will's old jacket.

In spite of the two-hour rule, Angelina had stayed at Lucy's for almost four hours, and as soon as she'd arrived home, she grabbed a trash bag and headed for the shower. The dead squirrel did not worry her; they had taken care of that. It was the maggots. Some of the little wormy things could have latched on to her clothes. Or they could be hiding in her hair.

Into the trash bag went her white tee, her black warm-up pants, her black sports bra, and underwear—she tied the strings, knotted them, then squeezed the air out and twisted the end around itself to form a giant knot. And into the shower went her body. She scrubbed, emptying the bottle of eucalyptus body gel. She washed her hair three times. Then she plunged into the tub.

She'd been eight or nine when she realized her mother did not leave the house, and it was around that same time that the bird had appeared in the garage. But with umbrellas opening into the Statue of Liberty, the Golden Gate Bridge, the Great Lakes, Angelina's world got bigger while her mother's kept getting smaller. First, her mother freely roamed the house, then only the kitchen and hall, her bedroom and bathroom. When Angelina left for college, her mother was thin and frail and no longer leaving her room. One day, her father called to say her mother had moved into the bathroom and was sleeping in the tub. Angelina had screamed at him to do something, to call somebody. And he'd cried. And then she'd cried. He was afraid if he forced her into an ambulance, she would break into pieces. Instead, she'd had a stroke right there in the tub.

The day after her mother's funeral, she'd spent over two hundred dollars on aromatherapy bath oils and scented bubble baths. She'd bought thick, white towels. She'd made herself take a bath every day for weeks. These days, when she was in the tub, only occasionally did her mother's death cross her mind. She reminded herself her mother was crazy. She was not.

Will came out and stood by the screen, his feet planted on the wooden planks of the floor. Angelina's were perched on the crossbar at the bottom of her rocker. She was moving the chair with her body. After her shower and bath and in the muted softness of the surrounding gray, she felt clean and safe. The only thing better than cloudy was the rain she'd grown to love as a child, when there was no pressure to go outside and everyone carried an umbrella.

Will sneezed, the sound hanging in the air for a beat too long.

"Bless you," she said.

Even with as dark as it was, Angelina could see how his eyes drooped, and she missed how they used to light up when she would appear and how they had lit up a month ago when she curled around him in the cabin by the lake after they'd taken Iris to school. She turned to the empty house and remembered the question Cara had asked over the phone earlier in the week.

"What does it feel like going back to work?"

"The same," she had said. "It feels the same."

"The same as what, Mom?"

"As every other day."

"But you haven't had a job outside the house in twenty years."

"I know."

Angelina took a sip of wine. She enjoyed helping Lucy as much as she'd enjoyed raising children. But it was the same.

And yet something had changed today. She wasn't yet sure what, only that something had.

Several large birds went swooping past, too quickly for Angelina to identify them. She thought it unlike herself to enjoy watching birds from this porch where they had attacked her, but as horrific as that was, at some point she'd realized that the attack justified a fear she had worried was craziness. And she became grateful. Now from the safety of the screened-in porch, the vividly colored bodies of the birds and their freedom mesmerized her. Last year, she'd even bought a field guide. She'd known that the blackbirds at Lucy's were crows because ravens were larger, their feathers more layered. A raven also tended to be by itself, but if ravens were ever in a group, they were called an unkindness. Which made sense.

Angelina glanced at Will, whose eyes now looked closed. She tried to put her glass down on the table in the wet circle she'd already made, but each try seemed to spread the circle out a little more. Now, she picked up the glass and intentionally set it down in a different spot. Then another one. The little wet swirls all over the table reminding her of the maggots. On that *60 Minutes* episode, they had showed how to use them medicinally, how they ate only dead flesh, ignoring tissue that could still be saved, something doctors could not always see.

After the medicinal maggots, without even a commercial break, Morley Safer had stood on the Atlanta Motor Speedway where Will Petty and Clemson University had created a Defensive Driving Program for Teenagers. She and Will had watched in amazement as kids intentionally put cars in a spin so that on a rainy Friday night, when it happened by accident, they would be prepared. A tiny girl with straight, blonde hair had said, "I'm such a coward. The first time I tried it, I let go of the steering wheel and screamed." But by the third time, a camera inside the car showed her gently turning in the direction of the spin. They interviewed the head of the program, who said, "Hands follow eyes." Angelina remembered that phrase. "If they're looking at the guardrail," he'd said, "invariably that's what they'll hit. We teach them to look where they want to end up."

Will cleared his throat.

Angelina untwisted her legs, forced her feet to the ground, and followed Will into the house, but she caught the door before it closed and looked behind her, through the darkness, to the mountains in the distance.

CHAPTER 16

After Lucy hollered that the door was unlocked, Angelina stepped inside to the familiar sound of Lady barking and the unfamiliar sight of Lucy bent over the kitchen counter. But seeing both Lucy's hands buried in what looked like roadkill, Angelina backed away.

"John Milton shot a deer," Lucy said with delight, raising a butcher knife and wiping her forehead, smearing hairy blood across it like war paint.

Angelina glanced behind her, above the door where one knife was missing.

Lucy, not looking up, said, "It's just the quarters. Won't take long."

Angelina dropped her tote and purse on the table, then took off an older black sweater she'd found in the back of her closet. After she settled into her chair, she extracted her bottle of water. These days she was always thirsty.

Watching as Lucy crissed and crossed, she said, "You seem to know what you're doing."

"Well, you have to let the meat tell you where to cut," Lucy said. "It's like Michelangelo. You have to see the thing in the stone."

Angelina's eyes darted from the bloody mass to the torn magazine pages taped to the wall. When she looked back to the kitchen, she saw the woman in the trailer.

Which made all sorts of things feel possible.

Then it sounded as if Lucy were breaking china, but she was just plopping pieces of meat onto a line of plates, which she then shoved into the fridge without wrapping in foil or plastic. Holding her bloody hands in the air, she moved to the sink to wash them, then leaned her face under the water too.

Angelina turned back to the pages on the wall, leaning in close to compare some of the before and after pictures. The only one she recognized was *The Creation of Adam*, in which Adam and God were reaching toward each other. She put her glasses back on to read that the workers were using a chemical treatment to strip away smoke deposits, oil, wax, and dust—time's accretions. The table shook as Lucy wedged herself into her chair.

Angelina stood and went through her tasks, taking Lucy's temperature at the same time as her blood pressure, which was still elevated. She made a note for the doctor, reminded Lucy that this was the halfway point of the visits, and asked if she had any questions.

"Do you have other patients?" Lucy asked.

Angelina closed the file folder and sat down. "You're my only one." She glanced at the wall again. "So you like Michelangelo?"

"Since third grade. My teacher Ms. Elyea told us about him. How he lay on his back to paint the ceiling of the Sistine Chapel in Italy. She set us up like that, taping paper underneath our desks. We laid down on our backs in that little space and reached up to paint. I loved the smell of the brushes—like gasoline—and I loved that feeling of lying in my own little spot and reaching for something."

In the trailer, other than the faded photos on the wall, there was no evidence of reaching for anything. But she noticed the hallway leading into the back. She'd never been past the bathroom.

"When I used to clean houses..." Lucy said and paused for a second.

Over Lucy's head, dirty dishes covered the counter.

"People threw away good stuff. Pretty postcards and magazines. I found those pictures in a trash can. I wanted to show John Milton the big world that was out there and all that was in it. And he taped them up right there."

Angelina looked again at the magazine pages on the wall.

"Of course, I wiped stuff off good if I kept it," she said quickly. "I love to clean."

"But Lucy, look around." Angelina glanced again at the dishes and also at the clothes and cushions all askew.

Lucy looked and shrugged.

"What changed?" Angelina asked.

"Nothing." Lucy's fingers picked at the plastic candy corn bag still on the table. She shoved three orange, white, and yellow triangles in her mouth.

"Are you hungry?"

"Food is the doorway to the self," Lucy said.

"Eating one sweet thing makes you want another sweet thing."

"Or sometimes a salty thing," Lucy said. "Do you love being a nurse?"

"I want to hear more about cleaning."

Lucy looked at her.

And Angelina didn't care.

"I love candy," Lucy said, and then popped in three more triangles, moving her tongue around, poking her lips out.

Angelina knew what Lucy was doing—sliding sugar off her teeth.

"I was so thin," Lucy said. "No fat anywhere. It made my mother crazy."

"Is your mother still alive?"

"Heart attack at fifty."

"I remember. You told me that the day we did the initial paperwork. Was she overweight?"

Lucy looked at her.

"Well, I'm just saying being overweight is a health risk. And you can change that."

Lucy patted her stomach and rubbed in circles.

"Does your stomach hurt?"

"My bed has a pine headboard that reaches around me and turns into a table on each side. It's like a friendly giant who has his arms around me."

Angelina sat back, resting her head against the wall. "I haven't spent time with anyone new in ages."

Lucy started to smile but moved her hands to her hips and rubbed in circles there.

"Are your hips bothering you?"

"The doctor said I would probably need to get the other one replaced too."

"Maybe not if you lost some weight."

"I used to clean a room so fast it would make your head spin. Before I got as fat as my mother. Before my hip broke. Do you like to clean?"

"I like to make order," Angelina said.

"I want to be able to swoosh around again," Lucy said, her hands going from her hips to her scalp. "What do you want now?"

Angelina smiled.

And so did Lucy.

Angelina looked at her watch and gathered her papers. "You know, to be able to move," she said, "you need to start moving." Then she stood and picked up her tote and purse and sweater. "Just open it up like this," she said, opening the door. "And walk on out."

CHAPTER 17

The door Will had salvaged from the trash pile across the street in front of Mary Beth's house now had a new life as his worktable. It rested on two sawhorses and, after sanding, was soft and smooth, no trace of its original black. Resting on the table was a small box, and Will could not stop staring at it.

Another damn box. Number five. He hadn't meant to. The pieces of poplar had been propped up next to the dumpster in the hardware store parking lot the day he bought the sawhorses. He'd thought he would make a tray for eating while he watched TV. The next thing he knew he'd cut a piece of wood four inches by four inches. Then he'd cut another the same size. All his boxes had tops.

He scooted his chair back and leaned over to put his face eye-level to the box. It was a beaut. Poplar was a nice, hard wood. Easy to work with. He sniffed. No smell. Creamy white on this side. He turned the box. Little streaks of gray. He picked it up and put it on the second shelf next to number four. All were the same size. All exactly alike.

Maybe he kept making them because he knew how to make them. He arched his back and surveyed the room. He stood still and listened. Nothing. Absolutely no sound.

He turned out the light and headed up the stairs that were now as familiar to him as his spot in the den. His keys hung conveniently by the back door on the wooden rack he'd nailed above the larger coat rack, both of which he'd made last week. He snapped the keys up, started the car, and went south on the Appalachian Highway, taking the same route as driving to the main Water Works plant in Kennesaw, only he didn't go quite as far. In under an hour, he pulled into the parking lot of the Best Buy.

The section that claimed to be Music was full of keyboards and guitars. He went back to the guy in the blue shirt and yellow vest standing by the front door.

"Where do I get what I need to listen to music?"

"Home Theater System. Over to your right."

"I don't want movies," Will said. "Just music."

"IPod or receiver?"

"Receiver." There was a word he understood.

"Home Theater System. To your right." Now the man also nodded in that direction.

The last time Will had bought speakers was right after college when he'd chosen the two biggest ones he could afford for his new stereo system. Now all the speakers were small and seemed to come in families of five. A young woman in a blue shirt was watching a man in a cowboy hat singing on a screen so huge the blue-shirted woman seemed a part of it. Her blonde hair hung on her chest in two braids. He liked braids.

"Excuse me," he said, and when she turned her cute face to him, he had to concentrate on his words. A music situation. For his workroom.

"How much sound do you want?" she asked.

"Regular," he said.

"Well, how big is the room?" She slid her hands into her back pockets, leaving her thumbs out. Cute thumbs.

"Probably eleven by eleven," he said, feeling as if he should do something with his hands.

"Karaoke or just listening?"

"Just listening." He put a hand on the shelf to his right.

"From a receiver or iPod or your computer?"

"From what. I hadn't really thought about that." He rubbed his usually smooth face and felt the first splinters of what he might allow to turn into a beard. "We have a stereo system in the den."

"Oh, when you said just your workroom, I thought you wanted an independent system."

"Absolutely," Will said. "Definitely."

"Well, what do you want to play? CDs or digital?"

This was way too complicated, and Will was tired of complicated. "I want something easy."

"IPod speaker dock. Small. Clean. Uncomplicated."

"Except I don't have an iPod."

The woman smiled. "That's where I come in."

Will smiled back. Angelina and the girls had iPods. "Do you think I should have an iPod?"

"Really? I've given all my CDs away. I like to travel light."

"But this is for a room, not for traveling."

She fingered a braid. "I meant I like to travel light through the world."

"Ah," Will said, and looked at his hands.

The woman pulled something out of her pocket and removed a crinkly wrapper.

Will stared.

She put it in her mouth.

"What is that?"

She took the stick out of her mouth and pointed the red sucker at him. "You've never seen a Blow Pop before?"

What he'd meant, of course, was why was she eating candy while she was talking to a customer. But he was trying to be polite.

"So you want to keep going or what?" she asked.

"Yes," he said, feeling as if he'd been caught doing something he shouldn't have. He wanted to make this woman like him, to prove he still could.

"So with an iPod, you'll download music onto it from your computer. You won't be weighed down by the physical CD."

Will's heart was beating fast. He didn't feel weighed down. He just wanted to listen to music in his workroom.

"You have a computer, right?"

"Sure," Will said.

"Well, if you want my opinion..." She put the Pop in her mouth and took it right out.

"Please."

"I think you should make the change."

"To an iPod?"

"That's what I think."

"I'll have to learn to use it."

"You want to do that anyway, right?"

Will grinned. "Sold."

When she bent down and opened the cabinet, her blue shirt rode up her back, and he could see pale skin, which would be so soft. If she'd just reach a bit farther...there was the lovely hollowed-out area he wanted to...

"Okay," she said, standing up. "Now for the speaker dock."

Will followed her, watching her butt cheeks move up and down in her jeans, the area of fabric that covered the hollow space wiggling back and forth. When she stopped in the next aisle, he almost ran smack into her. She pulled a white iPod out of another pocket. So many pockets.

She plopped the small rectangle of white and silver onto the dock and then they were listening to a song he kind of liked—boom boom boom baboomboom—good beat. *Pressure pushing down on me.* Will nodded to the beat. She commented on the bass as if Will could hear it too. He cocked his head. He thought he could. Then she took her iPod and stuck it in a different dock, calling his attention to the reach of its sound. Then in another and another. Boom boom boom baboomboom. *Pressure. Pressing down on me."*

"I don't know," he said. "Let me hear it in that last one again."

"I just love David Bowie," she said, her face bubbly. "And Queen. My friends make fun of me."

Um ba ba be. She moved her hand in the air as if she were playing the drums.

Why can't we give love that one more chance...

Her fingers and thumbs were undoing a hair band. Will couldn't move. Then they were unwinding a braid. She put the pink circle on her wrist. Will watched as the three sections of hair became visible.

Give love give love give love...

Then she undid the other one, setting this pink band next to the white circular dock. She shook her head.

Under pressure. Piano. Snapping fingers.

She turned her face to him, her cheeks bright pink. They had listened to the whole song. Finally.

"This may be my favorite song of all time," she said, running her fingers through her hair, causing all trace of the different sections to vanish.

"Mine too," he said.

Then he realized how ridiculous that must sound, as if he were copying her. Or worse—entranced by her. "What are the odds of that?" he added.

He chose that dock, ready for her to bend down underneath the cabinet and reach far into the dark space to retrieve it for him. Unfortunately, the box was right at the front. He only had time to casually lay his hand on top of the pink circle, palming it before he followed her to the next location.

Forty-five minutes later, after Stella—*how will I find you again if I have another question*—had taken him over to the computers and helped him set up an iTunes account and after Will had spent a little over $400, he was heading home with a bag not much bigger than his briefcase but with a heart that seemed to have expanded. As if he'd managed to open something he'd thought was closed.

The next day, while Angelina was at work, Will found an old end table in the attic, which he took to the basement and where he set up his laptop. The small bag from Best Buy was on the bed right where he left it. He'd brought it all the way down here because he didn't think it should be anywhere else in the house. Now he was afraid to reach into the bag. Afraid to feel the pink hair band he'd dropped in there as he left the store.

Which was ridiculous. He snatched the bag and dumped out its contents, his eyes immediately locking onto the pink circle. Will sat down. Stella was no older than Cara. And he loved Angelina. He wondered if she'd want to have sex when she got back from work. Unlikely. He stood and paced around his small room, trying not to look at the pink circle. Was that a hair tangled onto it? He crept closer and picked up the band between his thumb and forefinger. One blonde hair. A tickle that made his lips part. And so fast he almost didn't see it, he dropped that band into the last box he'd made, clamping down the lid, as if that single hair could sneak out and hurt him.

Music. Right. He knew what song he wanted first. Something about pressure. And give love, give love, give love. He remembered that part. They must have listened to the beginning twenty times. A leaf blower started up outside. Maybe he could search for the song. He went to the Google and typed with his pointer fingers: songs with "pressure." The last entry on the page. "Under Pressure" by Queen and David Bowie. She'd mentioned Queen, hadn't she? Wasn't he the guy who wore the black and white paint on his face? He put iTunes into the Google man. He followed the steps Stella had shown him, and before he knew it, he was listening to their song. *Boom boom boom baboomboom...*

CHAPTER 18

John Milton's red truck was parked in front of Lucy's trailer again, and now Angelina wanted to see him, wanted to see what he would draw up out of her. She turned off the car, stuck the mug she'd brought for Lucy inside her tote, and before putting her purse on her shoulder, grabbed her sunglasses. Four or five umbrellas littered the floor. All the girls knew was that she liked to collect them, and on her birthday and Christmas that's what they gave her. Her favorite from Cara—white with colorful polka dots—reminded Angelina of that children's book, *Put Me in the Zoo*, and the sequel she'd discovered at Square Books when they'd been in Oxford with Iris—*I Want to Be Somebody New!* She reached for that umbrella now and then popped open the polka dots in the triangular bit of sunny sky between the open door and the car.

As she stood, she saw three-fourths of John Milton on the other side of the umbrella, which she lowered and squeezed shut so she could see all of him.

"What's with the umbrella?" he asked in a voice she felt in her chest. He spit on the ground between them.

"To the side maybe?"

His laugh made her feel as if she'd just taken her sunglasses off, but she'd never put them on.

"Lucy wanted me to leave before you got here," he said, sticking his arms up under his shirt and pushing it out away from him.

"She did?"

"So I wouldn't confuse you."

"Confuse me?"

"Also, she said there wasn't enough room for three people."

No hair covered his sunburned nose or his rough lips.

"What do you do after your bit of charity?" he asked.

"It's not charity. I get paid."

John Milton picked at his teeth. "Damn bacon."

Angelina watched him, trying to relax her shoulders. She felt her underwear rolling up on one side. As if wiping off her pants, she reached behind to free it.

"Your underwear creeping?"

She looked down, turning the umbrella in her hands, shaking it open again.

"What's the matter? That I said the word *underwear*?"

Looking into his face felt as if she were looking over the edge of something, and she pulled herself back. "I guess Lucy's waiting on me?"

He shook his head. "Taking a dump."

Angelina stomped her foot and turned her back to him.

"What?"

"Some things you don't say to people you just met."

"Why?"

"It's not polite."

"That's what you want me to be, polite?"

Angelina half turned and stopped. She opened her mouth but then closed it, reaching out for her car to steady herself.

"All my mother talks about these days is you," he said, loping toward his truck. "I wanted to see what all the fuss was about.

I have to say, I'm not impressed." And he got in his truck and drove away.

Angelina continued to stand there and to hold onto her car that startled her by looking just the same as it had five minutes before.

CHAPTER 19

Lucy held the mug. "You bought this for me?"

"The hospital is selling them," Angelina said. "One of the patients designed it." The dark blue mug had a pink flower on the front and a bigger-than-life-size butterfly on the handle.

"It's beautiful," Lucy said, turning the mug around in her hands.

They sat in their regular spots at the card table—their little island in a sea of trash, dirty clothes, dishes, open bags of chips—and Angelina updated the chart. "Where's the purple bucket?"

"Oh," Lucy said, "in my bedroom. I didn't think you needed it anymore."

"I don't," Angelina said. "I just missed it."

Lucy grinned. "Friday, I walked. Out the door and to the street. Saturday, I did it again. Sunday, I did it twice. And yesterday, I made it all the way to the 7-Eleven and said hello to Gracie."

"Lucy!"

"I had to sit down on her folding chair. My heart was beating pretty fast. I did that coughing thing to squeeze my heart. Gracie brought me a cup of water and tried to make me call you. But I felt fine. She got a customer to drive me back."

Angelina pushed against her chair. "Just getting started is the hardest part."

Lucy put her arms around herself, cradling the blue mug in the crook of her elbow. "I said to myself, just open the door." She laughed.

Angelina did too.

"And when I stepped from the stoop to the grass, the wind was blowing, and the cars were racing by. And I wanted to go somewhere new. So I touched the street with my toe and then walked back. I thought well, that's enough excitement for one day."

"Wow," Angelina said.

Lucy smiled so that her eyes lit up. "And when I went all the way to the 7-Eleven, I tell you, I felt, I don't know, alive maybe, for the first time in years." She set the mug down on the card table.

"Lucy, I'm so happy for you." And Angelina was, but she felt something else too, something uncomfortable.

"This new hip is working," Lucy said. "And I didn't buy any candy at the 7-Eleven. Or donuts. I feel so good, I don't even want any candy."

Which made Angelina wonder about so many things that she stood up.

"Where are you going?" Lucy asked.

"Maybe it would help if we cleaned up in here, got rid of some stuff." Angelina used to straighten the girls' rooms when they were sick in bed. As if they couldn't get well in the midst of disorder. Her mother used to do the same thing for her.

Lucy picked at her ear and looked at Angelina with that odd look she had sometimes, as if no connection was being made.

"You can't bend over," Angelina said. "But you can direct me." She scooped up a shirt that was clearly John Milton's—had his dark hairs on it. Smelled like outdoors and sweat. "Don't you think John Milton's old enough to clean up after himself?"

"You think it's worth all this effort?"

"We can do it in layers—like a treasure hunt. You know, first let's find all the trash."

Lucy shrugged. "Okay," she said. "Let's find all the trash."

Angelina spied a small Walmart bag on the far side of the couch. "Look, Lucy, another Walmart bag." Angelina held it up as if she'd found the golden egg.

Lucy shrugged.

Angelina peeked inside—some kind of half-eaten sports bar, a stick of Walmart brand men's deodorant, and a receipt. Sports bar and receipt in a trash pile and deodorant on the card table. She kind of folded the bag, handing it to Lucy. "You never know when you might need another one."

Lucy put it on the table under the mug.

A large white trash bag that appeared used but was empty poked out from underneath the futon. Angelina began to fill it. "Do you have any baskets for dirty clothes?"

Lucy glanced toward the hallway and said, "I thought you said trash."

"For the next layer," Angelina said.

Lucy disengaged herself from her seat, then hobbled toward the back.

"Don't bend over," Angelina said. "I can come get it."

"Stay there," Lucy said.

Angelina put the dirty dishes on the kitchen counter and was building a pile of clothes on the floor. Lucy came back carrying a cardboard box, which Angelina loaded with clothes.

Lucy wedged herself back in.

In fifteen minutes, they had removed all the trash, which Angelina would throw in the dumpster on her way out, and all the dirty clothes, which were waiting in the box for John Milton to deal with. They had even gotten all the dirty dishes and food substances to the kitchen.

"Done," Angelina said, from the middle of the room turning to look in all directions until she came back to Lucy, sitting Buddha-like at the table. "Do you feel better?"

"I felt pretty good before," Lucy said, looking at her. "Do you feel better?"

Angelina fell into her chair. "I'm an idiot."

"It *is* cleaner and nicer in here."

"What you did for yourself was really great, Lucy. All that walking."

"I bet you do things like that all the time."

Angelina shook her head, putting her elbows on the table and leaning toward Lucy. "There's this couple at the gym. He wears dark socks with shorts. She wears barrettes and Keds." She stopped there, for the first time wondering what Lucy must think of her. Her face heated up, and her first instinct was to backtrack, to say *not that there's anything wrong with that*, to add that she had Keds in her closet and barrettes in her drawer. But she didn't. She looked around the trailer, feeling a heated pressure also rising from her chest. If she began to cover up here at Lucy's, it would be the end of something, something like hope that had emerged from she didn't know where. She managed to be still. She breathed. She let her words hang in the air.

And then like something her body wouldn't allow her to control, she said, "I call them Nadine and Francis." She put her hand over her mouth. She wanted to say *excuse me*.

"Have you known them a long time?" Lucy threaded a greasy strand of hair behind her ear. "Longer than you've known me?"

"I don't *know* them." Her heart beat faster. She felt alert. The heat and the pressure were dissipating.

"How do you know their names?"

"I made them up."

"Made them up?"

"I was on the treadmill. I was bored. She seemed like a Nadine. He seemed like a Francis."

"What do I seem like?"

"Like Lucy."

"Well, you seem like an Angelina." And she picked up a package of peanut butter crackers that was open on the table. She popped one in her mouth and patted her stomach. "I call her Henrietta," she said, and laughed.

Angelina felt a surge from her head to her misshapen toe she'd forgotten she had. Her skin tingled. As she laughed with Lucy, she felt good. Happy. Delightfully un-perfect. "Henrietta—I like that." And then, "I bet Nadine has lots of cats."

Lucy laughed. "What else?"

"That her panties come to her waist."

Lucy slapped her thigh. "Just like me—that's pretty good."

"Like me too," Angelina said, and she tipped her head back and laughed some more.

CHAPTER 20

But at the gym, in the face of matching clothes, mirrors, strutting, Angelina could feel what had loosened, tightening; what had opened, closing; what had uncurled, curling back. She reminded herself to breathe.

Halfway through her workout, Nadine and Francis appeared—and they came straight to the circuit training section where Angelina was. In five minutes, Francis had already kissed Nadine twice. The next time Angelina glanced their way, Francis was sitting on a machine watching Nadine exercise. Angelina watched too. Nadine never looked in the mirror or adjusted her clothes. She didn't hold her stomach in or wear makeup. She didn't even seem aware of other people. Neither did Francis. Angelina imagined Nadine handing Francis a pair of black socks and Francis helping her gather up bobby pins. She imagined Nadine finishing one Snickers and Francis passing her another one. No judgments. Nadine could be Nadine. They loved each other that much—so much that Angelina could see it.

Francis stood and touched Nadine's hand. She stopped what she was doing and took her other hand to layer it on top of his.

Will loved her. He did. And she loved him. But not like that.

She wiped the sweat off her forehead and moved toward the machine numbered nine. She felt someone beside her and looked up.

"Oh, sorry," Nadine said. "I moved out of order."

"You go ahead. I don't know what I'm doing." Angelina looked over her shoulder for Francis. He was heading into the bathroom. "I noticed you working out with someone," Angelina said, as she sat down on number ten. "Do you like that better than working out by yourself?"

"I usually work out by myself. I've been coming here for years, twice a week. But my husband just had surgery. The doctor told him to start lifting weights."

"Oh," Angelina said, lowering the bar into place. "He's your husband."

"When I told him he needed to do strength training, did he listen to me? Then he fell playing racquetball. Broke a bunch of bones in his hand and wrist. Found out he has osteoporosis. So he's supposed to do weight-bearing exercises. I've been telling him that for years."

"So now you work out together?"

"But he'll be going back to work soon."

Angelina stood. "Enjoy your workout." And she turned away so fast, she almost bumped into the hairless legs and dark socks that were Francis.

CHAPTER 21

Not that Angelina didn't like Bruce. Because she did. "Jungleland" and "Darkness on the Edge of Town." The whole Dublin CD. "Land of Hope and Dreams." *This train, oh this train.* No, it wasn't that she didn't like Bruce. But Will was obsessed. With his new iPod. And with Bruce. "Rosalita" over and over again. And some other song—*doom doom doom dahdoodoom.* All Angelina could think of was "Ice Ice Baby." But she didn't think that was it.

She leaned her head back and closed her eyes. When she opened them, she noticed the ceiling fan was not on as it usually was, and that there was something dark all over it. She got up and flipped the switch to make sure it was working, which it was. Will must have turned it off by accident. Now that it was on again, it looked fine. She turned it off. There was definitely something all over it.

Standing on a breakfast room chair, Angelina got close enough to see that the dark stuff was not dust but dirt. The fan was filthy. How was that possible—spinning every day as it did above them. But it looked fine when it was spinning. She would have to get the six-foot ladder from the garage to clean it, the one she'd been using on Black Friday to clean the top shelf in her closet moments before the back door had slammed—with Will inside the house instead of outside it. She looked around. It was almost time for the porch. She would have to clean the fan another time. Or maybe, now that Will was around so much, she would ask him to do it.

●

Thick fog lay heavy on the mountains, almost covering them, the sun lost behind it all. This day was going to blur into another night if she didn't do something. She jerked her feet off the rocker onto the uneven floor. Looking at Will, she said, "I want something."

"Like what?" he said, looking at her.

"I don't know. But not breakfast. I don't want breakfast."

"I think we've established that," Will said, smiling.

"Are you growing a beard?"

"Maybe," he said. "What do you think?"

"Too soon to tell."

A gust of wind swept across the porch.

"I don't want to play house," she said.

Will's smile disappeared. He stood and leaned against the screen, facing her, facing the house.

"You look sad and confused when I leave for work," she said.

"Well, I did kind of think you'd be around more," he said, pacing. Then he stopped. "You used to be around more."

"Jeez, Will, things change."

"I'm ready to go back inside," he said, standing there for some amount of time before the door rattled shut.

She raised her glass to her lips, but it was empty. She set it down and continued softly rocking as the last light disappeared. From somewhere out there came the ghostly clicking of a nightjar, a bird she had learned was more often heard than seen.

Later that night after dinner, they cleaned up together as they usually did. When Will came back in after taking out the trash, he said, "You need two new tires—front left and back left."

Angelina was wiping the counters, her whole hand on the cloth against the granite. "Passenger side or driver's side?"

Will, on his way to his chair, turned around and stopped. "What do you mean?"

"Which left?" she said, wiping crumbs into her hand. "When you're facing the car or in the car? She rinsed her hand and the dishcloth, wringing it out and draping it over the faucet.

But Will was still standing where he'd stopped. He was staring at her. "There's only one front left." Even in the low light of the den, his features were sharp.

"Okay, but I don't know which one that is."

"You're kidding, right?"

As if the ground were splitting, her legs trembled. "No," she said, leaning back against the sink for support. She crossed her arms. "If you'd just tell me if it's the passenger side or the driver's side, then I'd know which tires I need."

"You're telling me there's more than one left front of a car?" Will asked, raising his voice. "You don't really believe that. You just want me to use your words."

"I don't understand." The dishwasher ticked forward, but she felt as if she needed to go back, as if she'd missed a step.

Will spun in a tight circle.

She reached to the counter behind her, tightening her grip and then loosening it, rocking her body with the motion. "It makes a difference whether you're standing in front of the car or sitting in the car."

"No, it doesn't," he said. "Does a cow have a different left leg whether you're in front of it or behind it?"

"Well, no. A cow is like a person. With only one left." She let go of the counter, and her arms hung by her side. "A car is like a cow?" What else was she missing?

CHAPTER 22

Angelina had meant to get right out of the car, but the bright red truck was parked in front of Lucy's again, and she found herself staring at the blue fall sky wondering why she could feel her heart.

The door to the trailer opened, and John Milton headed straight for her. He opened her car door. "Why are you just sitting here?"

"I was waiting for you to leave."

"You wanted me to walk out of the trailer and get in my truck without noticing you?"

"Yes."

"You did not."

"I guess..." she said and looked away for a second. "I don't know what I wanted."

"That's exactly what you look like sitting in this car—a woman who doesn't know what she wants."

She took the keys out of the ignition, grabbed her purse, the sky-blue umbrella, and made a motion as if to get out of the car, but she rocked back into her seat. "You're in my way," she said.

"Exactly where I want to be," he said. "Why are you still sitting in the car?"

"Because I want to."

"You do not. Do you always say stuff you don't mean?"

She stamped her foot on the floor of the car. "I want to get out."

He grinned. "So, get out."

"But I'll..."

"The first time I saw you, you made me want to leave the bathroom door open."

"You didn't just say that." She looked away, undoing the Velcro on her umbrella as if she were about to open it in the car.

He slid over so that all of him stood next to the door—as if he were an extension of it. Then he moved in closer.

"People just don't say things like that."

"Why not?"

"It's not appropriate."

He shook his head. "There you go again. Is that what you want? For me to be appropriate?"

"I want to get out of this car without touching you."

"I believe," he said, "that that's something else you don't mean."

She looked away again. Then she put one foot on the ground, and as she stood, her face and breasts slid up his chest. And she felt something she hadn't felt in a long time, something that took her breath away and also pushed it into the farthest reaches of her body.

As she stepped toward the trailer, he coughed. "Now I see what all the fuss is about," he said.

She didn't turn around or pause. Perhaps appropriate was not all it was cracked up to be. And despite sensing him watching her, she felt light on her feet as she hurried to the trailer. When she heard her car door shut, she beeped it locked, still not looking back.

CHAPTER 23

"Tell me something I don't know," Lucy said.

"My husband was fired, and I took this job not for the money or to help you but to get away from the house I thought would be empty but is now filled with him. Also, on the way over here, I bought three chocolate bars."

"I meant about me. Tell me something about me I don't know."

Angelina smiled. Of course that was what Lucy meant. Angelina looked down at the chart in front of her, "Well, you were born on January 4th—1/4—and I was born on April 1st—4/1. We're mirror images. That's pretty cool."

"I meant like you did about Nadine."

"Lucy, I don't really know Nadine. I know you." Angelina looked around the tiny space that enclosed them. Card table, futon, kitchen, hallway, slatted closet doors, Walmart bags. She smiled. "Lucy, you've never been married, have you?"

"Henrietta hasn't *always* been with me."

"I didn't mean to suggest that," Angelina said.

"Every time I try to eat less, I eat more. And I *was* married. A long time ago. To John Milton's father. Room number eight."

"Room number eight?"

"In the motel."

"What motel?"

"The Sky View Motel. He would leave his drawings around the room. Sometimes I'd find them crumpled in the trash. They were on this nice, thick, white paper and had ruffles on the end where he tore them out of his book."

"How long were you married?"

"I always wanted a boy. My mother too, but all she got was me. I guess she passed that want on."

"You wanted a boy specifically?"

"I was going to name him Michelangelo, and as soon as I saw the drawings, I knew this was the father." Lucy looked out the window. "It was the boy I thought of as we wrestled in the sheets I'd put on his bed that morning, the sheets I'd change again the next day. But that night, as I lay there with the roots of the boy taking hold, I had a dream about a boy and his name was John. Not Michelangelo. I've never argued with a dream, and I wasn't about to start."

Angelina took a sip from the bottle of water she'd brought.

"It was four weeks later I asked him to marry me, when I knew I was pregnant. He said he would, but that he'd want the divorce too. A package deal."

"Oh, Lucy."

"That was fine. I got what I wanted. And he wasn't in any hurry for the divorce. He just wanted to make sure I understood it was coming. We lived with his mother—Vera—until John Milton was a year old. Then we split." Lucy rubbed her temples.

"Do you have a headache?"

"No, why?"

"You were rubbing your head."

"I guess I do that sometimes. Tell me more about Nadine and Francis."

"It's just that they're always together. I'd feel claustrophobic if I had someone following me around like that, someone who never gave me any space."

Lucy looked out the window beside her. "That might not be so bad."

"You were lucky. To get to live all these years by yourself."

"But I haven't been by myself. John Milton's been here."

A gust of wind shook the trailer.

"I was seventeen," Lucy said.

"When John Milton was born?"

"When I knew what I wanted."

"What about now?" Angelina asked.

"Now I want to be able to move around like I used to."

Angelina could hear the traffic on the main road.

"And it might not be so bad to have someone follow me around—even if he did wear dark socks. Someone like Francis who thought I was wonderful."

Angelina looked into Lucy's spongy soft eyes—blue, but not as blue as John Milton's. Her face was round and puffy. Wiry gray hairs stuck out from her middle part. She had large pores, sleep in the corner of her small eyes, and dark half-moons underneath. A grease smear and maybe strawberry jelly around her mouth. Crusts around her nose.

Angelina reached out her arm and then her finger to touch the red jelly, and at the touch, she felt Lucy's rough finger on her cheek.

CHAPTER 24

An hour later back in her garage, as she was getting out of the car, Angelina noticed the navy gash she hadn't realized was still on the wall. Iris had been a few days from getting her license when Angelina suggested she back the car out. Iris got it stuck on the wall where it wouldn't go forwards or backwards. She'd had to climb out the passenger side, and Angelina had had to climb in the same way. Iris watched from the doorway, in tears, as Angelina scraped the car an inch along the wall. In the end, they'd waited for Will to get home to figure out how to detach the car from the wall with the least amount of damage.

Now Angelina stepped inside the house and smelled bacon, but the smell didn't seem heavy like a blanket but lighter like a cloud that might move on along. One splotch of color sat at the table all by itself. Her eyes began to fill. Maybe she would try sitting in front of the placemat for a minute while it was just a placemat—without its burden of food or Will. But the closer she got to the table, the more she didn't want to sit. So she stood in front of it, looking at the layers of color that created the placemat, not feeling as good about it as she had hoped, instead feeling the car keys marking the inside of her tight fist. It was simple and it was clear. She wanted no part of the placemat's striped fringe reaching out from each of its sides. Her eyes flitted to the empty space where hers should be, to the windows, to a bird she didn't recognize bobbing on the sill, and then beyond.

●

A whir emanated from the basement. Angelina had so resisted Will's presence in the house that she hadn't even been to see his workroom. Down the stairs she went now, knocking first but she could hear a machine so she opened the door. He had taken the curtains down. An old door rested on two sawhorses. He was bent over something and using a small tool that was making a lot of noise and a tiny bit of sawdust. The bed was now in a corner. Pillows lined the wall, turning it into a couch of sorts. Pieces of old wood were stacked in several piles around the room. On top of the bookshelf, his new iPod sat front and center against a small rectangular speaker. On the shelves underneath were wooden boxes, cans of paint, varnish, brushes, and stacks of magazines. An unusual black table with flecks of color showing through—it didn't look like something Will would have made—sat right in front of her.

The machine went off. He turned in her direction.

"What's the matter?" he asked, raising his safety glasses.

"Nothing," she said.

"What are you doing down here?"

"Visiting you."

"I didn't expect you back so soon."

"I came straight from Lucy's."

"As opposed to?"

She pulled her sweater closer around her and folded her arms, both hands now making fists—one around the strap of her purse, the other around her keys. "The gym, errands, driving around."

He sat.

"Cool table," she said, reaching to touch it.

"Don't," he said. "The paint's not dry."

"Is this the one you're making for Cara—the one that used to be ours?"

"It is," he said, putting whatever he was working on down. "Angelina, what is it you want?"

She took a breath, and as she exhaled, she pulled the other chair out from the wall and slid it in front of him. She sat, having no idea what she was doing but knowing that, like at Lucy's, she had to be still. And when she was, she remembered the candy she'd bought. She opened her purse and took out the three chocolate bars. She put two in front of her and pushed one, clearing a path through the bits of sawdust and shavings on the worktable, toward Will.

"Why would you give me a candy bar?" he asked.

Angelina felt her shoulders draw in toward her neck. She knew it was the part of herself she'd hidden away that she was fighting for. And Nadine popped into her head. *Go ahead*, Nadine said. *Be Angelina.*

She looked straight at Will and tore half the wrapper off one of the bars. She took a bite. Creamy, rich chocolate flooded her mouth. She could almost hear the chocolate swirling around, softening her insides, reaching toward her outsides. She chewed. Her shoulders relaxed. She took another bite, watching Will watch her. When she finished the first bar, she started on the second. He wasn't moving. The flesh around his eyes was loose. Brown spots dotted his temples, larger than the freckles that used to be there. She definitely liked his new beard and looked into his eyes that she'd forgotten were a chestnut brown. Without taking her eyes off his face, she could see his hand feeling for his candy bar. He picked it up and unwrapped one end. But instead of taking a bite, he held it out to her, and without breaking eye contact, she slid off her old black sweater and handed it to him.

CHAPTER 25

Angelina was not sure what she expected after she showed Will a piece of the real her. Maybe that the clouds would part and the walls would come crumbling down. Instead, they had sex. Well, that was what it seemed like these days. Sex. Love was elsewhere. In their blood. In their bones. In their skin. In the air perhaps. Sometimes not in their words or gestures. Will loved her the same way she loved him—with a brain and an opinion. Eyes-open. After twenty-three years there was no need to make love. Love was not only elsewhere; it was everywhere. Their love had its own life now, regenerating on its own. In memories, in photos, in cards, in music, in books, in the breakfast room table, in the dining room table. Often in words and gestures. It was above them and below them. In front of them and behind them. It was in between them, the invisible super glue that held their world together.

After they put their clothes back on, they ate lunch together at the table with two placemats. When Will went back downstairs, Angelina opened the door to the hall closet and reached behind his golf clubs and the box of Christmas decorations she'd never put back in the attic to the large Target bag that held her candy. In the kitchen, she arranged it in the middle of the table as if it were flowers. Then she yanked it off the table. She didn't want

the candy where she was *always* looking at it. It should be out of sight so she had to think of it. She didn't want to turn into Lucy, did she? *Did she?*

She heard whirring and hammering from the basement. So what if Will came up? In the kitchen she aimed for the counter, where she emptied the bag. She brought two large cookie tins in from the laundry room and put the chocolate candy in the red one and the rest in the gold one.

"What are you doing?" Will asked, holding his coffee mug.

"Jeez, you scared me." This was good, she thought. Now she could prove she wasn't hiding the candy.

"I didn't mean to," he said, rinsing his mug in the sink.

"I just didn't hear you come up."

Will came around the counter and pointed to his feet. "No shoes."

As much as she breathed slowly, she could still feel pinpricks up and down her arms and legs, as if tiny sailors had emerged on deck in response to an alarm. *Enemy sighted*, they were saying to each other. *Nonsense*, she said to them.

"What's all this?" He put a hand on top of the red tin.

"I'm putting my candy up." *See*, she told the sailors. *As you were.*

"Your candy?" Will put his mug down and began to pry the lid off with the pads of his fingers.

The tin was from A Piece of Cake. Kate had sent her that delicious spice cake for her birthday.

"What's it for?" he asked.

"Me. When I want it."

Plain and peanut M&Ms, Junior Mints, Snickers—Will tipped the contents toward her as if she didn't know what was in there.

She looked at his face, and what she saw reduced her.

"You think you have enough?" he asked, with a short, derisive half-laugh, half-snort.

He was a mirror she looked into every day, and each time she looked there was less of her there. She was so much more than Will knew. But she couldn't see that person anymore—the image was too faint. What she needed was a new mirror.

"It's not really your concern," she said, yanking the tin out of his hands and replacing the top.

"Where did it all come from?"

"I bought it."

"Why?"

"I like candy. I like to have it around. It makes me happy." Angelina grabbed the gold tin before Will could touch it, putting both tins in the empty drawer underneath the oven where they used to keep the girls' plastic bowls and plates, the stubby kid silverware. Then she moved to the other side of the island, away from Will.

"Don't you think candy is a little childish?"

"No, Will, I don't," she said, sweeping off the sugar from the counter and into her palm. "I think it's what I like."

"It's not good for you."

She emptied her palm into the trash and moved toward the table. "You're the judge of what's good for me? You think all the bacon and eggs and sausages are good for you? And that tin of bacon grease you nurse like it's still 1960. Things have changed, Will. No little kids at home. No little family. You don't go to work anymore."

"So that's what this is about," he said, slamming the pantry door that wouldn't close all the way.

"How should I know what it's about? You started it." Angelina grabbed the top of a chair so she would not walk away.

Will had apparently found some sugar granules she'd missed and was making a great show of smashing them with his finger.

"It has to be about you, doesn't it? You finally come down to my workshop, but it wasn't to see me. Or to talk about what I was doing down there. Or to see what I'd made. No. It was to eat candy. Not one, not two, but *three* candy bars. I'm the one who lost my job, and you come down to my workshop to eat candy."

Battle stations, she heard the first officer cry.

He was right. She had been selfish, but it was about time. "Would it kill you to take a bite of chocolate between meals? To do something because I thought it was fun? After twenty-three years, I know what you like and what you don't like, what you think is appropriate and what isn't. I squeeze into those clothes every day." She looked out the back windows at the mountains that seemed to be taunting her. "I know better than to be myself with you."

"Be yourself? You're not yourself. You've gone crazy." He spit the words out.

She flinched inside, if not outside too. Will knew what that word did to her. She was not her mother, but she felt that old fear like a flash of fire, something she'd thought was extinguished, but there it was.

"You're having a midlife crisis," he said.

"A midlife crisis is not the same as crazy. And you're one to talk."

"And," he said, "on top of everything else, now I have a wife who eats candy."

"No, Will. You've always had a wife who eats candy." And with those words, the adrenaline evaporated, leaving her body slack and her eyes without focus. "I can't talk about this any longer."

She drifted into the hall, toward the steps, concentrating to lift her legs, visualizing her bed. But it wasn't *her* bed. She grabbed onto the wood rail at the top of the stairs and then released the stubborn hardness of it. Where could she go? She needed a place with a door and a lock and went through their bedroom heading for the bathroom. But it was Will's bathroom too. On her right, she saw the slightly open door of her closet and in she went. From the dark side, she drew the door across the rug like a line. She poked the brass lever to lock it. Then she crumpled onto the rug, curled up into a ball, and closed her eyes.

CHAPTER 26

Of course he had to apologize. He made it a point to apologize after he screwed up. It was the right thing to do.

But Angelina wasn't in their room or their bathroom so he opened the door to each of the girls' rooms and then closed each one back. Had he even been in this part of the house since they took Iris to school?

Will knew he'd heard Angelina come upstairs so he went back to their room. That's when he noticed her closet door was all the way closed. He knocked lightly. No response. Then he tried the door and felt the little tug of not giving. He stood there for a second, not at all sure he wanted her to open it, then he went back downstairs.

All the way to his workroom, where he was almost finished with the table he was redoing for Cara. He added a coat of varnish and then went upstairs to his chair in the den and turned on the TV.

When it came time, he wanted her to come to the porch like she always did. He turned off the TV, climbed the stairs, and knocked on the door. No answer.

"Angelina? Look, I'm sorry for my part of the fight. Will you open the door?"

His fingernails had gotten a little long, and he began to bite them down.

"Honey, we don't have to talk about it anymore now. Just come out, okay?"

He waited.

"We can get a glass of wine and sit on the porch. It's late. You've been in there a long time."

He didn't hear anything. He pulled his socks up.

"Are you okay?"

Not one single sound in the whole house. He straightened his pants around his waist and leaned against the wall across from the door. "You have to let me know you're okay or I'm going to force the door open."

"Leave me alone," she said.

At her voice, which sounded far away and as if it were coming up out of the fibers of the carpet, he slid to the floor, which was at the same time his legs collapsing underneath him and his heart being pulled closer to hers. He would never leave her alone. Not ever. Not for one second.

Hugging his knees to his chest, he sat there unable to speak.

Then he tried to stand too quickly—it had been a long time since he'd had to get up off the floor and wanting to be quick about it didn't seem to accelerate the process. Downstairs, he poured two glasses of wine and brought them back up. He knocked again. "Angel, I brought you a glass of wine. If you'll just open the door. We can sit here, and we don't even have to talk." He closed his eyes, hoping that would sharpen his hearing, but no sound at all. Not a scrape or a scratch or a breath. He swallowed, feeling a little panicky. "I'll just leave your wine sitting right outside the door. Okay? And I'll go back downstairs. Come down when you feel like it." He set the glass on the rug, but he couldn't get it steady. So he leaned it against the wall, directly across from the closet door.

Downstairs in the den, the empty porch hit him in the face. He turned toward the TV instead, fell into his recliner, and put the local news on so low he could only hear some of the words.

It got dark. He got hungry. He poured another glass of wine and went back up dark stairs, but her glass was right where he'd left it. When he turned on the light by his bed, it hurt his eyes, which he shut and rubbed. When she'd brought him the chocolate bar—he knew it was important, he knew she was telling him something not just about her but also about him. He could feel it, and he even knew how to respond in that moment, but he was also afraid she was losing her mind. He opened his eyes and stepped around the made bed into the hall, where he turned on the light. And then of course he'd been a jerk. But she was way overreacting. He leaned on the rail as he descended the stairs.

In the kitchen, he stood for a minute before he thought of heating a frozen pizza, which he ate sitting in his chair, watching the Braves in the last playoff game that he and Angelina had planned to watch together. At a commercial, he looked into the darkness and realized the phone hardly ever rang anymore. Before the game was over, he turned off the TV and all the other lights. He checked to make sure all three outside doors were locked, and also the one to the basement. Upstairs, he brushed his teeth, went to the bathroom, and got in bed. Often after a fight, Angelina let night work as a giant eraser. Maybe things would be back to normal in the morning.

But in the morning, she was gone. When he opened his eyes, she was not in the bed. He got up and knocked lightly on her closet door. It sounded looser. He tried the door, and it moved. No Angelina. He slung it all the way open. She was definitely not in there. The glass of wine still leaned against the wall.

He peed and then, without brushing his teeth, went downstairs calling for her. There was no coffee made, no bowl in the sink, no crumbs on the counter. The house seemed spitefully empty.

When he looked out the back door, her car was gone. *Well, I'll be god-damned.*

He stormed up the steps to brush his teeth and get dressed. Angelina always said he slept like a brick, but how could he not have heard her? By the time he got back downstairs, he wished he'd started the coffee the first time he was down here. He picked up the phone. She didn't answer her cell. And he didn't leave a message. He tried again. Same thing.

He had an idea. He picked up the phone again. Then he put it back down. *Where is Cara's number?* There it was—taped to the wall right in front of him. He dialed.

"Hi, Mom," she said.

"It's Dad."

"Oh, Dad, it's hard to remember it might be you calling from home on a weekday morning."

"Your table is ready," he said.

"Cool," she said.

"Since it's Friday, I thought maybe you and Quen could come after class? You could spend the weekend?"

"Dad, I'm meeting Iris at the football game tomorrow. I thought you were coming too. With your friend."

Damn. "I forgot all about that. Dan's picking me up at eight."

"You forgot about it?"

"It's just...I don't have a good system yet. For things like that."

"We could come after Legal Aid and stay for dinner," she said, with a lighter tone. "Will you make your cornbread?"

When the girls were little, to amuse them one Sunday when Angelina was out, he'd made a batch of cornbread—his mother's recipe, which called for the bacon grease Angelina refused to touch. He had fixed all three girls up at the table, each with her own kid knife and slab of butter and went off to make a quick phone call in peace. When he returned, the afternoon sun was squeezing through the windows, transforming itself into a blanket of hazy light that landed right on the girls as they huddled over the cornbread, gobbling it up as fast as they could get the warm, buttery, crumbly pieces in their mouths. *Why didn't I take a picture?*

After that day, it was *his* cornbread. Looked like it was turning out to be *his* kitchen too. He hoped it wouldn't turn out to be *his* house.

"And can we have steak too? But I gotta go. I have class."

Will hung up feeling much better. And he also had the game tomorrow to look forward to. How could he have forgotten about that? He wrote *Dan 8:00 a.m.* on a yellow square and left it by the coffee pot. He added *4 steaks* to the grocery list. The day was no longer veering off into space as it had been a few minutes ago. It had a shape.

The stairs were dark, but his workroom was full of light. He'd been smart to take the curtains down. He touched the edge of the table—dry. Then closer to the middle—almost dry. Surely it would be all the way dry by tonight. He looked around the room. He might as well go on to the grocery store. At least it wouldn't be crowded now.

By late that afternoon, he still hadn't heard from Angelina. It would be embarrassing if Cara and Quen got here before she did. He called her cell again and this time left a nice message that he hoped to see her soon and that Cara and Quen were coming for supper. Then he gathered the ingredients for the cornbread—first from the pantry and then from the fridge, staring for a moment at the vacant space he had created next to the skim milk.

He crowded the four filets onto a chipped plate—looked like all their plates were chipped—and doused them with Worcestershire Sauce and pepper. He washed the family of potatoes and left them drying on a paper towel. Back at the fridge, he took out the ingredients that would turn into a salad. And some raspberries. Cara would eat as many of these as he washed. The oven was preheated to 400. He checked the dishwasher. Empty. He picked up the rag that was right where he'd left it that morning, slung in a heap over the divider in the sink, and wiped the counters that even he wasn't sure needed wiping. Four colorful placemats from the drawer and four chipped yellow plates. Four napkins and four sets of knife, fork, and spoon.

He glanced at the stove clock, which seemed to be getting dimmer all the time. He made a note of that for Angelina and left it by the coffee pot, next to his note about the game. Four o'clock. He put the potatoes in the oven on the bottom rack and sat down in his chair with a tall glass of water to read the paper he'd neglected that morning. Cara would be here in an hour. Surely Angelina was planning on coming home. *Don't be ridiculous*, he told himself. They'd had plenty of fights before. Even if he left mad in the morning, by the time he came home—and he always came home—he was ready to move forward. And she was always here.

At four-thirty he folded the newspaper and laid it on the coffee table. He got up and made the cornbread, sliding the pan into the oven on the top rack. He returned the buttermilk to the fridge, to its spot behind the skim milk. Cara and Quen would be here any minute. He wondered if Angelina was still at that person's house. *Trailer*, he corrected himself. *Lucy's trailer*, he corrected himself again, afraid that Angelina liked this Lucy better than she liked him. At least she would be done with her soon.

One minute batter, the next bread. He raised his glasses to read the time. Five o'clock. The time Cara said they'd be here, which he knew was not the time they *would* be here. Apparently he was the only person in the world who could be anywhere on time. Hell, he was always early. It wasn't that difficult. Will cracked the oven door and put it on broil, a temperature at which he could not walk away or the next time he looked, the cornbread would be burned. There, it was done. With the potholder, he grabbed the skillet and set it out to cool. He turned off the oven but left the potatoes in. After washing the lettuce, he laid it on a paper towel to dry. Then the raspberries.

What was not to love about this sort of life? He was master of the kitchen. After pouring a beer, he zigzagged around the dining room table and chairs in the room where no one ever sat to the window that looked out on the street, so he could see Angelina's white Volvo at the first possible moment. He could smell the cornbread now, and it made the house smell like somebody lived here, like somebody cared. He'd always liked to cook. When he was in college, he'd thought about being a chef. His mother had pointed out the hours—nights, weekends—and to prove his mother wrong he'd worked in a restaurant kitchen the summer after his sophomore year. Instead, he'd proved her right.

Across the street, Mary Beth came out her front door. Will

darted behind the curtain. Why did she always come out when he was standing at the window? She would think he was nuts. He never dreamed Angelina wouldn't be home by now. And Cara and Quen about to be here. In the den, Will turned on the TV, flipped through the channels, and turned it off. He opened the door to the porch where it was pleasantly cool even with the sun still above the mountains. The trees seemed full, but the leaves were all brown and dead.

It was weird being out here by himself. It was weird being home by himself. He ran his fingers down the screen. He had built this porch to last. But he didn't miss being a water doc—he was past ready for the move home. But in an odd twist, now that he was finally holding solid *things* in his hands, it felt like his Angel, the solid person he'd been holding onto for years, was slipping through them.

He faced the house and saw the front door open, and before he could get to her, grown-up Cara in jeans and boots was hollering, "Dad." He gave her a hug and then spoke to Quen, who had on a V-necked white undershirt without a real shirt over it. Quen was a free spirit. Like their Livie. They both had a detached air about them, as if they floated from place to place, lacking any sort of docking apparatus. He and Cara had been going out for over a year. He liked trucks. Angelina liked him.

"Nice beard," Cara said.

Will rubbed his face.

"Where's Mom?" Cara put her purse and fleece down on the steps, as if she'd be going up to her room in a minute, as if she still lived there. Then Quen threw his fleece on top of hers.

"She's at that person's house," Will said.

"What person?"

"You know, her patient, Lucy."

"Now?" Cara looked at her watch. "It's almost five thirty. Wait, she told me she just went on Tuesdays and Thursdays."

"I'm always getting her schedule mixed up. Today's the office. Anyway, she should be back soon." Then he remembered what she'd said yesterday about not coming straight home. Where was she? He noticed Quen heading into the kitchen. "Do you want to go ahead and load the table?"

"Suits me," Quen said, turning around.

"I can't wait to see it," Cara said. "Is it in the garage?"

"Downstairs," Will said, leading the way to the stairs and flipping on the light at the top.

"Mom told me you had a workroom down here."

"In the guest room," he said, pausing and looking back. Cara was right behind him, her boots hitting each bare step. "Because of the light."

At the bottom, Cara said, "I can even smell your cornbread down here."

"Makes me hungry," Quen said, behind her, putting his hands on Cara's shoulders.

Will opened the door.

"Wow, the table looks awesome, Dad. And great room."

"Pretty cool, Mr. Brooks."

Will smiled. He had taken charge of this room just like he used to take charge of things at work.

"Dad, I had no idea you could make something like this."

A simple drop leaf with tapered rope legs—the first table he'd ever made. For their apartment. Angel had wanted a yellow table so he'd painted it yellow. It had sat in their kitchen against the wall, where they ate on it every day. When they moved into this house, she'd wanted a "real" table, so he'd sanded and stained it. When they needed a bigger table, this one had gone against a wall in the den. After that he lost track of it. He would notice it here or there. He'd found it again in the attic in August when Angelina asked him to take some boxes up. She'd spent the whole summer cleaning things out.

"How'd you get it all these colors?" Cara asked. "How'd you think of this?"

"That tie-dyed t-shirt. I can't remember how old you were. Your mother would wash it every night while you slept so you could wear it again the next day. I got pink, yellow, blue, green, and red paint. I let the colors drip and splatter. But then it looked like maybe I'd painted it for a six-year-old. So I got black paint and painted over the whole thing. Then I sanded it lightly so the colors showed through in places. And varnish."

"Very, very awesome, Dad," she said, giving him a hug. "I wonder whatever happened to that t-shirt."

"It's probably in the attic."

"These are cool too, Mr. Brooks."

Quen was looking at his boxes.

"I don't know what I'm doing with those," Will said. "They're not finished." He needed to get back upstairs where he could hear Angelina when she arrived. "Shall we take the table up?"

Cara picked up his iPod. "Dad, you got one?"

"I did."

"I've been trying to get you to buy an iPod for years."

"Well, I just decided I wanted to have music down here." He let down the leaves of the table.

"Good speakers on this dock, Mr. Brooks."

"Did you figure it out by yourself or did Mom help you?"

"Stella."

"Stella?"

"The woman who helps me at Best Buy. Ready?" He leaned over and put his hands underneath the table.

"You know her name?" Cara said, heading up the stairs.

He and Quen followed with the table. Halfway up, stuck behind Quen and the table, he heard the back door. *Damn it.*

"Cara?"

"Hi, Mom," Cara said, disappearing from the stairs.

"Why didn't you tell me you were coming?"

"Dad didn't tell you?" she asked.

Finally out of the stairs, and there she was. A little noise like a purr escaped, he was so relieved. He coughed to account for the sound. And only now was he willing to admit to himself what had been running deep through him—he'd been afraid she wasn't coming back.

He wanted to go to her, but between them stood the table, then Quen, then Cara—so he just stood there looking at her and also at Cara, who was looking at him. Angelina looked at Quen.

"Hi, Quen. No, he didn't tell me. I didn't realize he'd finished your table. Is that cornbread I smell?"

"I left you a message on your cell phone," Will said. "It was kind of last-minute." Quen put the table down, but Will kept hold of it. "I called to tell her the table was ready. After you'd gone this morning." He coughed again and tried to catch her eye, but she was not making direct contact.

"Can you stay the weekend?" Angelina asked Cara.

"Mom, we're playing Ole Miss tomorrow. Iris is coming on the bus. You've both known about it for ages. What's wrong with y'all?" Cara looked first to Angelina and then to Will. She looked at Quen who shrugged his shoulders, then back to Angelina. "We're staying for supper."

Angelina looked toward the kitchen. "Well, let's go see what we can dig up to go with the cornbread."

"I picked up some steaks and stuff for a salad," he said.

"Your favorite meal, Cara. How nice, Will."

She said this without looking at him.

"Why are you wearing exercise pants?" Cara asked.

Angelina looked down. "I went to the gym after work."

"The gym? You don't like gyms."

"Well, I thought I'd give them another try. We don't want to stand here all night. I'll hop in the shower, and we can sit on the porch. You aren't in a hurry, are you?"

"Not a hurry, no."

Angelina disappeared up the stairs.

"The gym?" Cara asked. "She hates to exercise."

Will held his arms out to his sides.

After they loaded the table into Quen's truck, Will lit the grill. Quen and Cara got their fleeces, and beers, then Cara grabbed a handful of wet raspberries and stuffed them in her mouth. They headed toward the porch.

"I'll be right out," Will said, chopping the onion. He would cut the red pepper too and then get another beer for himself. That whole scene with Angelina had gone well, he thought. He wondered about going upstairs but was afraid that might stir things up. Perhaps "space" really was the way to go on this.

When Will joined Cara and Quen on the porch, the cool air felt refreshing.

"This is kind of weird, Dad."

He knew it. All he had to do to confirm what he suspected was to bring in a third party.

"It's weird for you to be the one at home getting supper ready and Mom to come in the door."

"Not that there's anything wrong with that," Quen said to Cara.

"Of course not," she said. "It's just that all my life it's been the opposite."

"Things change," Quen said.

Will ran his finger up and down the screen. "I was tired of working," he said. But he had only wanted that one thing to change.

"I hear you, Mr. Brooks."

Will looked at Quen, twenty-five and in his third year of law school.

"I'll tell you what's weird," Will said.

Quen and Cara both looked up.

"What's weird?" Angelina asked, coming onto the porch smiling, a glass of wine in her hand, beautifully squeaky clean from the shower, her makeup gone, her home self back. His Angel. He leaned to kiss her before he realized what a risk he was taking, but she offered her cheek, which he accepted, and taking this as a positive sign, he added a squeeze around her waist. She had on the old gray jacket that she'd given him years ago, which had to mean she wasn't still mad.

"So what's weird?" she asked again, rotating away.

He watched her sit in the rocker next to Quen. "I can't remember what I was going to say. How was your shower?"

"Mom, I thought you hated exercise."

"Well, I'm starting to like it. Maybe it was just that I never had enough time for it. Or if I did, I was too tired." Angelina laughed.

Cara smiled.

The sun was still glowing but close to gone. With Angelina back, it seemed as if all was right with the world. "If only Livie and Iris were here, that would be everyone," Will said.

145

"Thanksgiving's in a month, right?" Cara asked. "Livie's coming back for that?"

"Five weeks from yesterday," Angelina said.

Why wouldn't she look at him?

"Dad, we need to figure out where to meet tomorrow."

"When does Iris's bus get there?"

"We could meet at halftime?" Cara proposed. "You can text me where your seats are. Then Quen'll help me find a place to meet. Mom, you sure you don't want to come? We could find you a ticket."

"It hasn't been that long since we dropped Iris off."

"Two months," Will said.

She took a sip of wine. He took the last gulp of his beer. Cara's and Quen's rocking chairs were creaking along together, but Angelina's was moving faster.

"How's Lucy doing?" Cara asked.

"Pretty good, considering. Did I tell you her son paints billboards? He's big—well, she's big. Wide, I mean. John Milton is tall, with big bones. Gruff. Black hair."

"You didn't tell me she had a son," Will said.

"Well, I've only seen him a couple of times," she said to Cara. "He reminds me of a bear."

"They live in a trailer," Will said.

"I've never known anyone quite like her."

"So you like working?" Cara asked.

"I do. I didn't expect to. But yes."

Will turned back to the view. How fast it goes, he thought. How could it be that what he'd gone to school to learn to do, he was done doing? That in fact he'd had a hand in bringing it to a close. Of course he hadn't thought he'd be a water doc until he died. Just for the rest of his life—something that used to stretch out in front of him.

"Will?"

He turned to her.

"Should we start dinner?"

"Sure," he said. "Nothing to do but the steaks. Stay out here if you like." He opened the door and then paused, looking behind him for the sun that had already disappeared, seemingly taking with it the sense of purpose he'd felt all day. For the first time in a long time, he felt like he needed some sugar. But the difference between him and Angelina was that he knew the feeling would pass. He was just hungry, and they would soon be eating.

Cara stood. "We'll all come."

He went on in, wondering how long he'd been standing there, half in and half out, and if Cara now thought he was the one acting weird.

On his way to the grill, he heard her ask who wanted water. He stuck his head back in the kitchen door and said, "I do." Cara smiled at him, and Angelina looked his way. He waited a moment hoping for something more. Then Quen called Cara from upstairs to see if she could help him find a copy of *Siddhartha*, Angelina turned back to the salad, and Will closed the door.

Siddhartha was a book he hadn't thought about since high school, but he could still see that blue cover. He let the garage door up. When he went around the corner to the grill, a gust of wind came off the ridge that made him wish he'd grabbed his jacket. He turned to face the house. This part, at least, seemed normal. Him outside by himself cooking on the grill. Angelina in the kitchen. Water that he made safe being put on the table. But he didn't make the water safe anymore. He coughed and looked down at a fallen yellow leaf. He covered it with his foot. He should have suggested they eat in the dining room. When he looked back up, it was just dark enough so that what he saw through the small kitchen window appeared not only framed but illuminated—as if it were something else he should take a picture of.

CHAPTER 27

Angelina told Quen and Cara goodbye at the door, and when Will followed them out, she went up, getting in bed quickly, and turning off the light. When she heard Will come into the room, she didn't move.

A little after midnight, with their windows open as they were almost every day of the year, she heard the rain begin. It had been a while, and she'd missed the rush of water, the release. She fought sleep, wanting to hear every splash, but the sound relaxed her and she slept. Later, in the early morning darkness, along with the rain, she heard the insistent wails of a train whistle. She turned on her back. Had she been dreaming? And then there was the whistle again, longer, a plea almost. She wondered what it would be like to go somewhere just as day was breaking, the rain slanting against the windows.

Even as she wondered, she knew she couldn't leave. Will would never understand. If only she could love *and* leave.

The next thing she heard was a radio announcer blaring from Will's alarm. Then the weight of him leaving the bed. She closed her eyes, thinking back to closing them the night before last in her closet.

Lying on the floor with the door locked had felt as if she were giving up. And perhaps she had for a bit. But when she heard his voice and responded, "leave me alone," she knew she hadn't, that she was just retreating in order to fill the well. In the early morning hours, she had opened the closet door as quietly as she could and tiptoed out of the bedroom, as she could hear Will tiptoeing out now on his way to the game. When the door clicked behind him, she rolled to the middle of the bed. She could not see the thing in the stone. She didn't know where to cut. She didn't know how to carve away what didn't matter to get to what did.

Yesterday morning, she'd gone from her closet to the car, driving to the Dunkin' Donuts out by the Interstate, pretending she was on a trip by herself. Perhaps she was pretending to be who she really was.

In the drive-thru, she'd ordered a half dozen hot, glazed donuts, a carton of milk, and the largest coffee they had. She'd pulled into a space in the parking lot and eaten three of the gooey donuts without a pause. Then she'd leaned back in her seat, the lard coating the inside of her mouth, the sky beginning to light a new day. What if she had no one to consider but herself? What if she had day after day to do only what she wanted when she wanted to do it?

She *was* selfish. To the bone.

She rolled over and kicked off the covers. She loved them all. She didn't understand this craving to be by herself.

Her legs ached. She reached down and rubbed her calf. Yesterday she had spent hours at the gym, walking on the treadmill. Hours. *One foot in front of the other.* The same words she'd said to Lucy she had said to herself.

Nadine had come in—without Francis, who had gone back to work. Was she happy to be by herself now? Angelina had asked, the two of them side by side on treadmills. She *was* happy, she said; still when he was here, she was happy too. She was one of those people who pretty much took life as it came. Although back in the day, she'd had a little trouble when they couldn't have children. She suspected it was his fault. His brother didn't have any children either.

Angelina had assimilated so many of Will's rules: She no longer adjusted the light after he had gotten used to it; she no longer watched TV in bed; she never invited the girls into their room for the late-night conversations she remembered from her child-hood; she never asked Will for something she could get herself. Her face heated up. Her whole body felt hot even without the sheet. Sometimes it was hard to know where she stopped and Will started. Maybe she no longer liked to watch TV in bed either.

On her back, she stared at the dark ceiling that appeared to be getting closer. All those sneezes that demanded to be blessed, all the thoughtful offers that required replies, the yawns, the chewing, the crunching. She was trivial and petty and preventing herself from seeing beyond.

Opening her eyes, she pulled the covers up. She wanted the feel of them on her body, but they constricted her movement. Her long toe pushed against the sheet. What if there were no house, no rules, no frame? Again, she kicked at the covers. Each of the girls could take care of herself. Will could take care of himself. It would not be shirking her duty. She could, in fact, leave them all behind. So either what she needed was courage or leaving wasn't really what she wanted to do.

CHAPTER 28

For the first time since *the nine days*—with Will in Athens for the football game—the house would be empty the whole day. Angelina sat at the dining room table staring at the sideboard, the only other piece of furniture in the room, and then at the only other things in the room—pewter coasters and silk flowers in shades of rose, echoing the still life behind them. The china and crystal were out of sight, locked in a corner closet. It was a room full of space. No one's room and everyone's. With her finger, she traced the partial circles. Years ago, Will had played ping-pong with the girls on this table. Angelina hadn't thought there was any way the tiny, air-filled balls could be harmful. She took another sip of coffee. The marks weren't so much circles as tiny broken curls, reminding her of the maggots.

In front of her was the small foyer where the stairs led up and the door led out. That morning when she'd taken her clothes off, all she could think about was the future. So different from this morning. She'd swear even the air felt different—as if it were thinning, sharpening.

She'd stood in this very room in front of these very windows without any clothes. She hadn't wanted to be seen but had wanted the courage to show herself. Courage, there it was again.

In one week, it would be Halloween. In four and a half weeks, they would all gather around this table for Thanksgiving. Angelina left the room.

In the kitchen, she refilled her cup and felt no need to do anything about Will's note. Instead, she opened the drawer where she'd moved some of the supplies from the phone room upstairs, and she pulled out an unused spiral notebook. Sitting at the table, she held a pen above the ruled lines, and when the pen hit the paper, what came out was the word *BUT*. In all caps. Nothing else. Just B-U-T. She stared at the three letters. Not the beginning of a sentence—the middle, the response. *But, then, so.* She'd forgotten what it was like to be the one to start the sentence.

In the spring, when Iris was accepted at Ole Miss and the planning began for *her* new life, Angelina had become conscious that there was still something inside her, something she must have wrapped in tissue, hidden away, and guarded—with one of those locks that had a thick metal loop that swung like a door, one like she used to have on her locker in high school. But back in high school, she hadn't known anything was inside. She was just blowing around like rust-colored sea foam.

She got up. The mountains were bold against the clearing October sky. It had stopped raining, and the sun was trying to come out. She grabbed her jacket off the coat rack Will had put up by the back door. Five hooks, as if he could freeze time. As if by nailing exactly five hooks by the back door he could keep them all nailed to this house.

On the porch she put her hand flat against the screen, letting it absorb the cold air directly through the tiny holes. She could see her breath this morning. Then she moved her other hand to the screen and finally she pressed her face against the copper mesh until she smelled metal and felt the marks of the minuscule openings on her cheeks. She became again the little girl standing at the screen door, looking out at her father's car, trapped inside because of a small thing.

She felt pressure underneath her eyes and began to walk the length of the porch as if counting off its feet for some sort of measurement. She watched her shadow get bigger and bigger until she crashed into it. Over and over again. Stop, she told herself. Be still.

She brought her feet together and let her arms hang loose. She relaxed her shoulders and breathed out. What, she asked herself. *What?*

Angelina heard the honking before she could see where it was coming from. And it wasn't the different pitches and overlapping squawks of a flock but single honks with pauses in between and getting closer. There it was. Not the V-formation she was used to seeing, but a lone Canada Goose late on its way south. The goose came more into focus, got bigger and bigger, and looked as if it were heading straight toward her. Instead of fear and instead of fleeing, as the goose soared higher, Angelina felt possibility, and as the goose curved to the left, Angelina's upper body spiraled with her. And then the goose was over the house.

Angelina untwisted herself so that she was again looking at those mysterious smoky blues. Her life was not some movie where the door to herself opened only during a nine-day period and then closed forever. She could make it happen, just like the goose.

Look where you want to end up, she thought. Hands follow eyes.

And Angelina looked harder than she'd ever looked before, now seeing the top of the continuous, rolling mountains in front of her as clearly as black against a white sky. She thought about what stood between here and there, and that sometimes what was in your way was not in front of you but behind you. She swiveled around.

Kitchen. Breakfast table. Den. House.

Angelina stared at the rusty door in front of her. Not just in front of her but in her way. She took hold of the tarnished knob, watching her wrist roll to the right. She pulled. Inside, she surged to the back door and opened it, adjusting the little brass clip on the closer so the screen would stay put. She felt the stale air disperse. On that outflow, she reached across the threshold and around the corner to raise the garage doors. In the kitchen, with both hands as if she were parting a curtain, she opened each side of the pantry. She took the key from the kitchen drawer to unlock the china closet in the dining room. She flung open the large front door, letting it hit the wall behind it. Upstairs she opened the door to the phone room, again with more force than was necessary. Then the doors to each of the girls' rooms—one, two, three. She slid her closet door all the way into the pocket and, without pausing, ran down the stairs, swung around the banister, and in front of the door to the basement, came to a hard stop.

This door was massive and solid, with dark waves in the stained wood. Knotty circles. Indentations. Her fingers started at the burnished hinge and traveled up and down its soft surface, over the ridges, all the way to the other side where the worn brass knob begged her to reach for it too.

CHAPTER 29

When Will came in the back door sporting his bag from Best Buy, a coffee from Running on Empty, and a pair of her shoes he'd found in the middle of the garage, Angelina, in her black and white work-out clothes, glanced his way and smiled. She picked up the egg carton, opened it, and began filing away the eggs.

"Where should I put your shoes?" he asked.

"Just right there, by the door."

He arranged the shoes facing each other under the coat rack. Then he went to Angelina at the fridge and kissed her dry lips, his bag crinkling between them, his eyes open, hers closed. He thought about smashing the eggs up against her, rubbing the yellow yolk onto her breasts.

"I'll be right back," he said.

On the way to their bedroom, he stepped down hard on each step. Not one word about what was in the bag or where he'd been. And this time he wasn't going to tell her. She would have to ask.

In the bedroom, he unboxed his new clock with the A and B alarms that Stella had helped him set. He unplugged his old squat alarm clock that he could no longer count on. Had he ever used another one? When he plugged the round one in, the correct time magically appeared in large blue digits, WED at the top.

"Isn't it cool that it just automatically knows?" Stella had asked. "Every time I plug one in, it just knows. So like I said, you can have one alarm for work. And one for the weekend."

She looked at him expectantly. "So seven for the weekdays," Will said, clearing his throat.

Stella pressed a button on the side of the clock.

"What time do *you* get up on the weekend?" Will asked.

Stella looked at him.

"How about nine for the weekends?"

"Nine it is," she said. "Boy, I wish I could sleep 'til nine."

Will had changed his mind about which clock three times so he could watch Stella's shirt ride up her back, her skin emerge, and then that space between her butt cheeks he wanted to fill with his finger. He'd had to thrust both hands in his pockets. Young Stella, with each of her braids flopping on a breast, had showed him how he could hook his iPod to the clock too. He had coughed then to dislodge the image of her in bed, next to him. He coughed again now, sitting on his bed, with the small round object she'd held in her hands on his night table, next to where he slept. He stood, adjusted his pants, and dropped his clunky old clock into the brown paper bag he kept in the back of his closet for stuff to take to Goodwill. Then he went downstairs—all the way down, swinging around the banister like Rick, and ignoring the noises coming from the kitchen.

In his workroom, Will took the seven boxes from the bookshelf and lined them up like the days of the week, one after another across the edge of the worktable. He was hoping if he saw them in a line instead of on two different shelves, he could figure out why he'd made seven small boxes, all just alike. He sat on his chair backwards, as if he were mounting a horse. Or Stella.

He coughed again.

The late afternoon sun fell across box number five. He wrapped his arms around the back of the chair and propped his chin on top.

The same, the same, the same. He was so boring. Except, he remembered—how could he have forgotten—one of them contained Stella's pink hair band. Maybe not so boring. He pushed against the back of the chair. Stella.

Will glanced at the empty space where Cara's table had stood. Angelina's footsteps swept across the den floor overhead.

He was not a woo-woo sort of guy, and yet he felt like the boxes were trying to tell him something. It was unusual for him to make the same thing over and over again. He stared, thinking about the empty space inside six of them, the pink circle inside one.

One thing he knew.

He didn't want to make any more boxes.

CHAPTER 30

As Angelina got in her car to drive to Lucy's for her next-to-last visit, John Milton was on her mind. It wasn't the first time she'd thought about him since he'd stood in her way and she'd chosen to rub up against him to get by. And she shouldn't be thinking about him in that way. He was too young. In relation to her. And more importantly she hadn't thought about anybody but Will in that way since she and Will got engaged. And besides, she wasn't looking to have a thing; she was looking for empty. Well, empty wasn't the point.

As she got close to the 7-Eleven, she began to look for John Milton's red truck. Then as she got close to the trailers, she noticed that one was missing. How odd she'd never asked Lucy who lived in the other two. And that she'd never seen anybody else around either. Not odd really. Anything she had in her mind as she got out of her car vanished as she stepped inside Lucy's trailer.

But when she got closer, she realized it was *Lucy's* trailer that was gone, and her heart felt as if it might pop out of her chest. It made no sense. Lucy wouldn't leave without telling her. She jolted to a stop, grabbed her purse and tote in one swoosh, got out, and beeped the car locked. But then she stopped. Not only had she parked in the giant rectangle of discolored empty space that used to be filled with trailer #1, but she was also standing in it. She ran her hand through the air, half-expecting to come into contact with something she merely couldn't see.

At the door to trailer #2, Angelina stepped on the cement block and knocked, trying to decide whether to ask for *Lucy* or *the woman in the trailer* or... when she heard Lucy call out, "It's open."

She pushed on the door and stepped inside. There Lucy was, still here, and lying on a futon, her face splotchy. Angelina had that same feeling as when one of the girls finally walked through the door an hour after curfew. She took another step to the middle of the room, turning in a circle. It was all the same—a carbon copy of the other trailer, only everything was nicer, and newer, and clean, and it smelled like oranges. She was unsure which question to ask first. "Are you okay, Lucy?"

"John Milton's gone."

"Gone? Wait a minute. He stole your trailer?"

"It's a home. A mobile home. And he just mobiled it off this morning. It was gone when I woke up. Two days before Halloween." Lucy covered her face with her hands. "He took Lady."

"He stole your dog too?"

"I'm all by myself now."

"Oh, dear," Angelina said, sinking into her spot, which had become a nice, wooden chair.

Lucy's eyes peeked through her fingers.

"Lucy, how did you get inside *this* trailer?"

Lucy shot her a glance.

"Home, I mean. Mobile home."

"There's a hole in my heart now," Lucy said.

"He came in unannounced. He left the bathroom door open. He ate your food. And now he's stolen your trailer. Home. And your dog." Angelina wondered who she was trying to convince.

Lucy started crying and her foot moved as if she might be getting up, but it was only moving to help her turn face-in to the futon.

Angelina glanced out the window at the remaining trailer as she put her stuff down on a real table. "I'm sorry," she said. "I'm sorry John Milton's gone. Do you know where he went?"

Lucy cried harder.

"Why don't you sit up? I can make some tea." A box of tissue that looked just like the one Angelina had given Lucy a while back sat in the middle of the table as if it were a decoration. Angelina pulled a couple out and dropped them next to Lucy's face.

This trailer was cozy, and it was all the space a person really needed. It was so...sufficient.

Lucy blew her nose and wiped her hands on the tissue, then began the process of sitting up.

"Is it okay for me to use the kitchen?"

Lucy nodded.

There were no dirty pots or dishes in the sink. In the first cabinet Angelina opened, she found cleaning supplies. In the second, shiny pots and pans. She filled one with water and put it on a burner. In the third cabinet she opened was the blue mug she'd given Lucy. Angelina picked it up and took it over to her. "Lucy, whose home is this?"

Lucy put her feet on the ground and pushed herself all the way to sitting. "Mine."

"Well, whose was the other one?"

"John Milton's."

163

"John Milton's?" Angelina asked, sitting down. Of course. "Lucy, why did you tell me that was your mobile home?"

"I don't believe I did."

"Well, why did you let me believe it? Why did we clean it up? Lucy, the squirrel."

"How do you think John Milton's doing?"

"Has he gone like to another state?"

"He bought some land. Somewhere around here. But he wouldn't take me with him."

"Then I think he's doing just fine. Probably at work, right?"

Lucy turned to her. "He would be at work, wouldn't he?" She picked at the tiny scab on her elbow.

"Lucy, quit picking at yourself."

"I can't stand things that stick out—like scabs. I like things smooth."

"That's why you never let me go in the bedroom, isn't it? I would have known it was John Milton's trailer."

"That's why I like watercolors. I can't stand the roughness of oils. You know how they can cake up?"

What would be next? Lucy unzipping her fat exterior? Angelina stood and went back to the kitchen.

"Are you having some too?" Lucy asked, hobbling to the table.

Lucy's voice not only rose at the end of the question, but it also hung there—expectant. Perhaps they were passing hope back and forth as needed, and it was her volley back to Lucy.

Angelina turned to the cabinet and took out a yellow mug. "That tea I brought you?"

"The cupboard to your right. Over the stove. I put it in one of those Ziploc bags you brought, along with that fake sugar."

Angelina opened the cabinet and there was the Honey Vanilla Chamomile tea and the Stevia packets. As she fixed their tea, she heard Lucy moving around. "Milk or no milk today?"

"Today I feel like milk." Lucy wedged herself into her corner spot at the table. She leaned her head back and exhaled.

Angelina removed the milk from the clean fridge and poured a splash in each of their mugs. She set their tea on the table and sat down, her hands around her mug.

"I don't know why I didn't tell you," Lucy said. "You assumed it was my place. And then...I don't know. It felt like protection, to meet you there."

So many things were falling into place.

Lucy looked out the window. Her mouth quivered. "I felt safe when there was a home on each side of me. Like how I feel in my bed. They were giant arms around me. Now I feel like one of the arms has been cut off."

Angelina patted Lucy's arm, then sipped some of her tea, the taste of it filling her body with warmth. When she put her mug back on the table, a little sloshed out. She reached for a tissue and dotted the spill. Then she spread the tissue out in front of her on the table and separated one sheet from the other so that she had two very thin tissues instead of one. She tore one of the tissues in half. Then she took one half and tore it in half. And as she was tearing that piece in half, she said, "Oh my god."

"What is it?"

"My mother used to do this—all over the house. I haven't thought about it since she died. If she wasn't cooking or watching TV or cleaning, she was shredding a tissue. She would do it just like that—each piece in half, again and again. That's how I knew to do it that way. Each little pile always had sixty-four pieces in it. For a while, I counted each pile I came across." Angelina dropped her forehead to the table.

"Two fingers of tequila," Lucy said. "My mother's remedy for everything. Stomachaches to the flu. The bottle's in the kitchen, in the cabinet above the fridge."

Angelina stood as if Lucy's giant were pulling her up from the middle. She found the bottle and grabbed two clean cartoon jelly glasses from the cabinet where she'd found the mugs. She plunked a glass down for each of them, the bottle in front of Lucy.

Lucy poured into Angelina's glass, then measured. Two fingers exactly. After she poured the same for herself, she threw her head back but only drank a little. Angelina felt as if she could see the clear liquid sliding down Lucy's throat, landing in Henrietta.

"Ah," Lucy said and laughed. "He's gone and I'm okay." She raised her glass.

Angelina raised her glass too and took a sip, pressing her tongue to the roof of her mouth.

"I'm really okay," Lucy said again, staring into the jelly glass. Then she said, "Catfish didn't believe in the power of two fingers."

"Catfish?"

After Lucy tossed her head back again, only one finger was left. "John Milton's dad. That's where the Milton came from, but nobody called *him* that. Even his mother called him Catfish. She was a piece of work. You could smell Vera everywhere. Can't stand the smell of violets even today. She died in her violet-smelling bed."

"I like the smell of violets," Angelina said, having another sip of this liquid that was just a bit heavier than water.

Lucy gnawed on her thumb. "I hated that house—it was so big. That's how I knew I wanted small spaces. Like under my desk the first time I had a brush between my fingers."

"My mother died in the bathtub," Angelina said.

"She just dropped right under the water?"

Angelina laughed. And she hadn't laughed about her mother in the longest time.

"No water."

"No water?"

"My mother hadn't left the house in years when she died. Apparently the bathtub was the only place that felt safe to her."

"Damn," Lucy said.

"Every time I came home, she would say these four things in a row—*Where have you been? It's not safe out there. Don't touch anything. Wash your hands.*" Angelina could see her mother's tissue droppings all over the house. The first thing she would do when she got home from school was scoop them into the trash. Then, wash her hands.

Angelina forced herself to swallow more of the liquid that tasted like woods. The light was shifting—it was only a little after eleven but felt later.

Lucy took a swig. "Catfish insisted I give the name to the boy. I wasn't budging on John, on account of the dream. Don't you think John Milton Craft sounds like poetry, like the name of an artist?"

Lucy was staring at something Angelina couldn't see. She seemed focused and not focused at the same time, as if what she saw was too big to be in any one spot. Angelina wondered how Lucy knew about poetry. And then she wondered if she would ever in her life stop judging people. She wanted her first thought to be compassionate, not her third. And then she wondered if she would ever stop judging herself.

"Lucy, how are you who you are?"

"What do you mean?"

"I always fall short."

"Short of what?"

"Short of who I want to be."

"But you are you—that's who you are. I love me. Do you love you?"

Angelina looked from Lucy to the jelly glass, which she turned toward her. Wile E. Coyote was suspended above a cliff, forever about to drop into the canyon below, his face only at that moment understanding.

"Lucy, do you remember the first time I came, when you said you thought I was going to ask you about your dreams?"

Lucy cocked her head.

"Why did you ask me that?"

Lucy took a John Wayne swig and emptied the glass. "You looked like you had some underneathness to you."

Angelina waited for more.

"I thought you might want to know if I had any to me."

"Do you?" Angelina asked.

"Do *you*?" Lucy asked.

There they sat—across from each other, fingering their empty jelly glasses, not breaking eye contact, grinning.

"Two more fingers?" Lucy asked.

"I'll take one," Angelina said.

"Anyway," Lucy said, pouring. "I told you his drawings were what drew me to him, but Catfish was in the mobile home business. Cash poor and mobile home rich. John Milton and I got one with the divorce and two new ones when he turned twenty-one."

"The other one is yours too?"

Lucy nodded.

"Who's in there?"

"It's empty."

"Empty?"

"It's perfect. Untouched. Nobody's ever lived in it. I tried to give it to John Milton, but he wanted the one he'd always lived in, the one we lived in together when he was growing up. Sometimes I go into the empty one and just sit."

Angelina closed her eyes for a second, imagining what it might be like to have a place of her own where she could sit by herself—how peaceful it would be, the pleasure of it. But she didn't really know what it would be like. She didn't know the truth of empty, the truth of alone. Her chest pressed against her heart, and she looked out the window at the empty white trailer that no longer looked dull. When she looked back at Lucy, she was picking her teeth.

"You know, if I was stranded on a desert island," Lucy said, "I could probably live for a week on what I pulled from between my teeth."

Angelina laughed. "Lucy, that is disgusting. But I know what you mean." She rested her hands on the table. "So you're all set for your appointment with the orthopedic surgeon on Thursday? For the six-week check on your hip."

"John Milton's taking me. He's getting off work."

"They're also going to do a blood workup. Then we'll do the discharge visit on Tuesday."

Lucy nodded, looking out the window.

"I'm going to miss you, Lucy. Maybe I could come by when I'm in the neighborhood."

"Or maybe you could come see me on purpose?"

Angelina grinned. "I'll do that."

"When John Milton was a boy, he used to make little signs for me. I've got them around here somewhere. In a box. Or maybe a drawer. You know the first time I gave him one of those small packs of crayons, he peeled the wrappers right off the crayons. He didn't want anything covering up the sticks of color. He did the same thing every time I'd give him a new pack. He told me he wanted to feel the crayons in his hand. He still does that."

"Have you lost weight?"

"I squeezed a whole bunch of that lemon you brought me all over the broccoli, and I did like it. John Milton wouldn't eat it though."

"Lucy, it's not about John Milton. It's about you."

"After he was born, I lost all but three pounds. Each year, when I went to the clinic for my pap smear, I'd gained three pounds. I didn't think that sounded too bad."

"Hardly worth mentioning," Angelina said.

"Times thirty years."

Angelina sat still for a second, amazed at what the years could do to a person.

To a couple.

Then she pulled the scale out of her tote and put it on the floor. She had not weighed Lucy since that first day when she admitted her. She would do it again next time for her discharge.

"My clothes do feel looser," Lucy said as she balanced on the metal square in her sweater and slippers. "I probably just need to wash them."

Angelina looked at the number and then sat back in her chair. "Lucy."

"What?"

"You've lost seventeen pounds."

"Seventeen pounds?" She sat down. "In four weeks?"

"Well, I think so. Let me find the file." She leaned over and rummaged in her tote, isolating the bent manila folder and pulling it out. "Okay, yes. Seventeen."

"What do I weigh?"

"199."

Lucy smacked the table. "Jesus God. I haven't been under 200 in years." Her eyes were wide. She looked so much younger.

"You are now."

"Angelina, think what we've done."

Angelina wasn't sure Lucy had ever called her by name. She raised her glass and said, "Lucy, to what *you've* done."

Next time, she would ask about her dreams.

CHAPTER 31

On Halloween night, Will and Angelina took their usual places on the porch, but she felt different—ragged and uneven, as if ice were breaking apart inside her.

Will wore khakis and loafers without socks, his navy V-necked cashmere sweater over a t-shirt. A baseball cap covered the top of his head where his hair was thinning so that, except for the beard, he looked just as he had years ago.

She took a sip of wine and said, "I noticed you bought a new alarm clock."

He smiled.

"Why?" she asked.

He stopped smiling.

"I mean, why now?" But that wasn't what she'd meant.

"You've made fun of my old one for years," he said, looking inside to the kitchen. "And I have this woman who helps me at Best Buy."

Good for him, Angelina thought. She didn't want him to be sad and was relieved some other woman was being nice to him. It was a weight off her shoulders. She sat up straighter and breathed out the deepest breath she had since he'd retired. Then she began to rock, staring out at the mountains, at the new spaces—the result of fallen leaves—almost like a path all the way to as far as she could see. "I like your beard," she said. "I really do."

He smiled again. "Livie called this morning while you were at the gym."

"How is she?"

"She doesn't want to come home for Thanksgiving. She wants to stay over there and travel. I told her we already had the ticket, that she needed to come home like we'd planned, but that I'd talk to you about it."

"Why does she have to come home?"

"It's Thanksgiving," Will said.

"She's in France."

"She's been in France."

Angelina dipped her body back and forth. The rocker picked up speed. "I always said it didn't make sense to buy the ticket for Thanksgiving, for her to come all the way home when she would only have a month left." Angelina stood and the rocker sailed back, knocking into the house. "She's twenty, Will. You know as well as I do that after she has a job and a family, she'll *have* to be home for Thanksgiving."

"We're always all together on Thanksgiving. Everybody else will be here."

"But it's not going to stay that way. Let it change. The girls are out in the world now, having their own lives. If they get married, their husbands will have families too."

"France is not the same as a husband's family."

"Will."

"Angelina."

"Don't you think you're being selfish?" she asked.

The doorbell rang. Angelina didn't move. She could feel Will looking at her. He got up and kicked the porch door and then opened it. She listened to him stomp to the front of the house and do what they were supposed to, what she refused to do any longer.

CHAPTER 32

That night, Angelina woke at four with a cramp in her extra-long toe that would not fall into line as it should, that during the day, pounded against the end of her shoes. She wiggled her toes, flexed them, and turned over facing Will's new alarm clock with the bright blue numbers. 4:03. At this strange hour of the night, she missed that old fake wooden one. She might as well go ahead and go to the bathroom. She would never get back to sleep until she did.

When Will woke at four, Stella disappeared. He closed his eyes quickly, but she was gone. So was her open mouth and her tongue on the red Blow Pop and her butt crack that he'd been reaching out to touch. He sat up and put his feet on the floor. After a minute, he headed to the bathroom. A moving shadow.

He started, his hand on his chest. "You scared me to death."

Angelina passed him without touching him, moving toward the bed.

CHAPTER 33

The week before, instead of throwing them away, Angelina left three overripe bananas on the counter—Will had said he wanted to make banana bread. After a few days, though, fruit flies. She took the rotten fruit outside to the trash. Still, the fruit flies continued to multiply. Time for the bug man.

Rick bustled right in as usual and headed straight for the kitchen, spraying along the baseboards even before his feet made it into the room. Angelina came behind his tall, lean body, watching it glide around. He stopped to spray inside the over-sized trash drawer and stopped again to spray into the disposal, a fruit fly's favorite hiding spot, he said.

"Have you seen any in the cabinets? he asked.

Angelina shook her head.

Then he looked up.

Following his gaze, she saw a line of fruit flies sitting along the edge of the top of the cabinet—small black angels looking down from above. "Uh oh," she said.

Rick opened the cabinet and stood back to look a good two feet above his six feet to the top shelf.

"Oh my god," she said, her hand moving to her mouth.

Rick set his canister on the ground.

There, on the top shelf, were the remains of red netting, calling to mind the net bags they sold on the side of the road in the summer. And then she remembered buying a bag of Vidalia onions early in June and placing it on the top shelf because the onion drawer had been full.

Now, slow-motion dripping over the edge and down the side of the cabinet was a tar-like goo that could easily have been congealed Worcestershire Sauce, except that it wasn't. Above it all, layer upon layer of fruit flies.

Rick scooted the stool next to the cabinet. "Bring me some newspaper," he said. "And do you have a heavy-duty trash bag, like for leaves?"

She and Will opened this cabinet a hundred times a day—or maybe twenty times a day now that Iris was gone. How could they not have seen this? It was impossible and yet it was true. If Will had discovered it and told her, she wouldn't have believed him.

"Mrs. Brooks?"

Angelina jolted into action, so relieved she hadn't found this gigantic monster while she was alone. She couldn't wait to tell Lucy.

CHAPTER 34

Will had given her the massage gift certificate that his secretary had sent him as a retirement gift—*For your new life*, the card read. Angelina made the appointment for the second of November, thinking that would be a nice way to start this particular month, and now she was opening the door to a small house.

"Welcome," a very thin, and very young, pregnant woman said.

"I'm Angelina."

"I'm Cile. The room is ready."

Angelina followed Cile into a short hallway, past a closed door and a bathroom and into a dark room, where soft music played along with the sound of water from a brook or a stream. A bed sat in the middle of the room, one corner of the blanket turned down.

"Have you had a massage before?"

"First time."

"Well, undress to your level of comfort." Cile had on a purple tank and a black tank, and over those, a tight, black, long-sleeved yoga top that hung halfway over her hands.

"Do I leave on my underwear?"

"Whatever makes you comfortable."

"What do you suggest?"

"Clothing is a barrier to relaxation. It's saying no instead of yes. The fingers need to be free to move. You'll start face down, your face in the cradle. Gerhardt will be with you in five minutes."

"Wait a minute. Gerhardt?"

"The massage therapist."

"I thought you were."

Cile smiled. "I'm the receptionist." Then she closed the door.

Angelina was definitely against barriers. She was also afraid of being caught half in and half out of her clothes. Which she ripped off. Then she unhooked her bra and stuffed it inside her purse and pulled her underwear down and stuck it in with the bra. When she'd called to make the appointment, Cile had answered the phone. Angelina had just assumed. The light green sheet peeled back like skin, and she crawled under the covers that felt clean and cool, and smelled of eucalyptus. As she settled her face in the cradle, she felt the years of taking care of others falling off her shoulders.

A knock on the door. "Are you ready?"

His voice was deep, and he had some sort of accent.

"I'm Gerhardt," he said, coming into the room. "Let's make you a little more comfortable."

In one motion, he lifted Angelina's feet and whisked a pillow underneath. He turned the sheet down low on Angelina's hips and stood above her head. Then he placed both expansive hands on her shoulders. He extended his fingers and let them rest there.

She could hear him breathe in and out. And she breathed in and out.

With both hands glazed in oil—scented with juniper she thought—he slowly pushed from her shoulders all the way down her back until he reached her hips where again he breathed in, and as he breathed out, he locked on to each hip bone and pressed his palms as if he were trying to disengage her hips from her back.

She felt parts separating and space being created for the first time in a lifetime—which was such an unexpected and welcome feeling that she felt close to tears. And she thought of Lucy and her hips, finally understanding why she had needed a new one.

Gerhardt's fingers traveled back to her shoulders, and he started all over again. The third time, when his palms reached her hips, the tips of his fingers reached just below the sheet.

Their first Thanksgiving after they'd moved into the house—Cara was four months old—she and Will had invited his mother who came all the way from Chicago, and Kate who brought someone Angelina couldn't remember, a couple of neighbors who had small children, and Will's boss Harry and his family. They had borrowed card tables (not having a real dining room table yet) and used different china and silver at each one, as if each table were its own little island. She had cooked, arranged flowers, polished silver. That night after everyone had gone, she remembered to soak all the white linen napkins in the laundry room sink with a little Clorox, something her mother had taught her.

Gerhardt was burrowing into an area below her right shoulder bone. He circled, getting closer and closer to a bubble of pain, until he landed on it, where he stayed, seemingly working with the bubble instead of against it. Then he went to the middle of her low back—as low as he could go—and then lower, finally working his way back up and circling the bubble again.

The morning after that first Thanksgiving, as soon as she stepped from the stairs to the hall, she had felt water on her bare feet, and she'd known in an instant—she'd left the water running in the laundry room sink. It had seeped out the door and also apparently under the wall, the wall not being a real barrier. They'd had to move out of the house for a month while the floors that had just been finished were refinished, walls that had just been painted, repainted. Their homeowners' insurance paid for everything—except the two-thousand-dollar deductible. So they took no vacation that year. With Cara in a snugly and with wet feet, Angelina had cried and mopped, at what she had done to herself, at what she had done to them.

Gerhardt unfolded the sheet from her hips and pulled it up to the top of her neck. He stepped to one side and folded the sheet in toward the middle of her body, exposing one edge of her—shoulder to foot. His fingers started at her hip and went up to her shoulder, and then down to her hip again and into her leg—waking up parts of her that perhaps had never been awake. And then his fingers slid down her leg and took her foot apart, releasing her long toe to take up as much space as it needed. His fingers moved up her calf, into her thigh, removing knot after knot, until finally it was the full sweep again shoulder to foot, foot to shoulder. He covered that side up and moved to the other.

Several years after the flood, the destructive power of water forgotten, Angelina stood in their backyard, staring at what had started as intermittent drips, became constant drips, and was at that point water gushing over the roof of the house. She had suspected a stopped-up gutter but was stupid to wait so long. Now there was a three-foot stretch of wood where the water had rubbed off the paint. There were rust spots and streaks down the shingles.

Gerhardt lifted the sheet and held it in front of his face. "I must ask you to slide down and turn on your back." After she did, he let the sheet fall over her, and then he stood by her head again. He rolled the sheet to the middle of her breasts, but she wanted him to roll it all the way to her waist. He started with one shoulder and worked into her collar bone before moving to the other. Always the balancing. His two large hands held her skull, cradling it, and with complete disregard for her hair, his fingers circled from the top of her head to the base of her neck where the tension hid.

Over the years, most of the repairmen she'd known whistled. Not Maxie. He was a Dave Matthews fan and sang their tunes. Angelina always recognized which one—because of the girls. As he emerged from the side of the house, "Ants Marching," she said. He winked at her. "You've got a gusher all right." But it hadn't been the gutter or a leak; instead, a stopped-up air conditioning line, the condensation overflowing out of the pan and down the side of the house. Maxie kept insisting it was working right. "That's what it's supposed to do," he said.

Gerhardt's fingers were still.

Angelina was still.

And it was in that moment of stillness that she saw herself sitting on top of the rusted paint drum at Lucy's, her new self stepping a foot outside the old, her toes testing the water.

Gerhardt, with his hands on her shoulders, bent close to her ear. In a whisper he said, "Your pelvis, hips, and femur were all locked up. Normally I have time for more. But I had to make a choice. You should feel much more ease of movement. Namaste." He closed the door behind him.

A long breath escaped naturally as if Angelina were used to such breaths. Breaths from so deep inside herself, she could feel her body and spirit struggling forward, each with its separate task but each pulling the other along as it could. Today, her body had arrived in a fist and Gerhardt had uncurled her, had rolled and rolled and rolled until Angelina not only had stopped curling in but also was ready to open out.

CHAPTER 35

Will had forgotten there was so much about water in *Siddhartha*—how it flowed and flowed but was always there, how it was the same and yet every moment, new. He'd forgotten about the river. He questioned whether he'd ever even read the book, which he'd found on a bottom shelf in the den, wondering if Quen had forgotten it or if they'd never found it.

Glancing toward the porch, he thought about today being Angelina's last visit with Lucy, and he wondered if there would be some sort of drama associated with that. He also wondered if it were possible for Lucy to somehow force another round of visits.

In the kitchen he added coffee and water to the coffee maker, but then he just stared at the empty pot. In the dining room he watched Mary Beth stretch, pulling one leg up behind her. As she bounced down the sidewalk, she waved to him. Maybe he was a peeping Tom, and he knocked into a chair to get away from the window.

Surely there was something he needed from the Best Buy. But in the car, on the way, he couldn't think of anything. Except he did need something. And Stella had *something*. Something larger than life. That was it, a little dose of vibrancy. That was all he needed. He looked at his watch. Almost noon. No wonder he was hungry. Maybe he could take Stella to lunch.

Once there, he hurried to the glass doors, nodding to Mr. Man in the yellow vest as if they were old friends. He knew his way around and went straight to Stella's area.

But no Stella.

His heart thudded into his brown loafers. How could he not have considered this possibility? Maybe she was in the bathroom, or on an early lunch, or working in another part of the store. He wandered around, looking up and down each aisle. Go to the source, he thought, heading for Customer Service, explaining that Stella had helped him before and knew what he wanted. Where was she?

A boy with pimples exploding on his face didn't spend nearly enough time checking the computer in front of him. "Off today," he said. "Would you like me to find someone else to help you?"

Will turned and headed straight for the door, blowing by Mr. Man, who wished him a nice day. Will yanked the door to his 4Runner so hard it hit him in the thigh. *Get a hold of yourself.* But he skidded out of the parking lot and onto the highway, having no desire to slow down for food.

He turned on the Boss and tried to settle down. The next thing he knew he was in the National Forest, the last fifteen minutes before home. Just as he was coming out of the trees, "The Promised Land" came on, and he turned up the volume, and for the first time in twenty years, he didn't want to stop driving. *Driving across the Waynesboro County line I got the radio on and I'm just killing time. Pretty soon little girl I'm gonna take charge.* He turned up the volume again and kept going. He played the steering wheel as he sang. *I believe in a promised land.*

Staying on the Appalachian Highway, he headed east across the state—his weekly drive years ago when he worked in the field.

This was the drive Harry had wanted him to start making again, but adding other drives, promoting him to cover the entire state and to be the company liaison to the surrounding states. No damn way.

By the outskirts of Blairsville, he was starving. He circled the courthouse and was getting ready to park in front of the Hole in the Wall when an elderly couple, arm in arm, stepped into the space into which he was turning. He hit the brakes and waved them across, smiling to reassure them, noticing as he smiled how the wife leaned her head onto the husband's shoulder.

Once inside, Will ordered a fried catfish sandwich, a slice of rhubarb pie, and a sweet tea to go—just like the old days on the way to the headwaters except five years ago all the waitresses knew his name. If he didn't stop until he was on the way home, he'd sit down at one of Jean-Ann's tables, and she'd put in his order for a Two-Egg Mountain Breakfast with Two Hot Cakes on the side before she brought his black coffee, all such a treat back in the days when he never got to eat breakfast at home. He'd slip her tip right into her little apron pocket, his fingers maybe lingering a beat too long. Today he didn't recognize either of the waitresses. He glanced at his watch—1:45, no wonder the crowd was thin.

In the car again, he sat back in his seat, getting expansive with his legs. Then he dropped his lunch on the passenger seat. He knew where he was going, and he advanced with purpose. From here, he'd get on the Gainesville Highway and in another fifteen minutes, hit the 180 Spur. He found "The Promised Land" and played it again, louder, wondering how The Boss got to be The Boss.

Regular people parked at the Visitor's Center, but he pulled off on the wide gravel shoulder where the trail crossed the road, no other cars like always. Will's hiking shoes were still in the car—he'd never taken them out. Hell, the trunk was where they belonged. And there was his green cooler guaranteed not to leak. He moved it to the front seat so he'd remember to take it inside when he got home. Leaving the tea and grabbing a bottle of water he found on the floor and his lunch, off he went, straight up and into the thinned-out woods. It would be good to get more exercise than just his morning walk. Good to be out in the wild again. To get his heart pumping.

As he hiked, he noted overgrown areas and soaring hawks. Fall was the best time for this hike, though he'd missed the high point, the leaves now crunching under his shoes. He scanned the path for footprints, not finding any but other people had been here. The cool air was bracing, invigorating. Up and down. After ten minutes, he took off his jacket. Birds, squirrels, even mice— he always saw more wildlife on this trail than any other. He was starving now but wouldn't eat until he got to his spot. Another fifteen minutes and he was at Chattahoochee Gap with the familiar blue sign and white W needlessly pointing him toward the headwaters. Two hundred feet and he was there. A gentle spring that would become a river and push forward over five hundred miles to the Gulf of Mexico. The small beginning of the mighty Chattahoochee River, and he had not a test tube on him. He laughed out of pure pleasure.

Today the spring was full of fallen leaves, but the water didn't seem to care. It flowed around them and over the rocks. After peeing off the trail behind a tree, he tossed his jacket on a rock and sat down on top of it to finally eat. He was sweaty and his back was stiff, but he felt good. Hiking had been a regular part of his work in the field, and he'd missed it. He especially liked loop trails where he didn't have to backtrack, which he'd have to do

15

today. His catfish sandwich was better than he remembered, the tartar sauce soaked into both sides of the homemade sourdough roll.

Anyway, he was glad not to be the one in charge of the water anymore. He'd only been getting through each day by telling himself he would retire as soon as it was decent. He didn't want to expand; he wanted to contract. He wasn't in a rut; he was in a groove. A groove down the other side and headed for home.

His work had come from the need to do the right thing. And he had done that. Out the wazoo. Until after they'd taken Iris to college. And then, after all these years, Will had chosen in favor of himself.

He closed his eyes and arched his back. He opened them and the spring was still there. A light wind blew through the trees, bouncing the branches. A squirrel ventured onto a rock, and Will watched it watch him. Squirrels were such stupid creatures. If they'd just stay at home eating nuts or at least on their side of the woods, they wouldn't be flattened running out in front of cars as they dared themselves to cross the road. And they wouldn't fall from ceilings into sinks.

He wasn't bitter about all the years of work. He was proud. But it was time for him to get what he was supposed to get in return. He wanted what he'd counted on, what he was entitled to. Getting out of bed when he wanted, spending time with Angelina, helping around the house, being a grandfather instead of a father. Doing things his way. Letting people come to him. He was looking forward to the TV, to the paper, to naps. To being crotchety. To saying who could come into his house and who couldn't. He was looking forward to turning into an old man. It was his due.

But Angelina seemed to want something else. And they used to be two people who wanted the same thing. He picked up a stick and in the dirt drew a face, her shoulder-length hair.

All he wanted was to be at home and to spend time with the Angelina he knew—the one who used to look at him in the same way that Stella did. And he was so close. He could make it happen. He was sure he could.

CHAPTER 36

It was time to make her last visit to Lucy, but Angelina felt as if she were trudging through thigh-high water. She couldn't find her keys; she caught every light; Lucy's new prescriptions weren't ready, and she had to wait. Instead of four weeks, it seemed like years ago that she'd first knocked on that aluminum door.

As her tires bumped over the curb, she thought the absence of the third trailer did leave Lucy exposed. There was nothing between her and the street. Angelina looked around, feeling a little exposed herself, too full and at risk of spilling over.

It was a cold, motionless morning. No birds. No wind. She wrapped her arms around herself, drawing her coat tighter as she took the few steps to the trailer. She knocked and missed Little Old Lady's barking. She turned to face the 7-Eleven. No cars.

She'd waited on the cement block before, but Lucy always hollered to say she was coming. Angelina knocked again. Nothing. She put her ear to the door. She trailed her fingers down like rain. Then she straightened and knocked longer and harder, her knuckles stinging. She stepped off the cement block and looked from one end of the trailer to the other. In the cold silence, she could see her breath. Maybe Lucy was in the empty one. Angelina waded to the eerily similar trailer, all the while looking for some sign of Lucy. She wasn't tall enough to see in a window. The thin curtains were all closed anyway.

It *was* Tuesday, right? She checked her cell phone. And it was ten.

The door to the trailer marked #3 shined. Not a dent or a smudge. As Angelina knocked, she wondered if Lucy cleaned it. She called out her name. No response. As she returned to trailer #2, she looked toward the 7-Eleven where a black truck was now parked. Maybe Lucy had gone over there to surprise her. She'd just knock one more time, then head over. Actually, she should probably take her car so she could drive Lucy back. After knocking, she called out several times, then turned toward her car. She wished Lucy had a phone. Three crows cawed from a nearby tree. A buzzard landed in the street next to a bloody mass.

"Lucy!" Her name pierced the air as Angelina lunged for the door and grabbed the doorknob, first jiggling it, then jerking it backwards and forwards. Surely she could bust through it. She turned sideways and leaned her weight against it. Nothing. She stood back. If only the cement block were not there. She was going to kick the door in anyway. But what if Lucy was at the 7-Eleven or had gone to visit John Milton? So Angelina would buy her a new door. She stood back and kicked, praying she'd be buying Lucy a new door. She felt the door give a bit. She kicked again, making a dent the size of her heel. She thought this might work. On her third kick, the door flew open.

"Lucy!"

She was wedged into her spot, her head tilted back against the wall, her arms on the wooden table, her eyes closed.

Angelina bolted to her and grabbed her stiff wrist from the table to check for a pulse she knew she wouldn't feel. Then she sat. The smell was not bad yet, a little worse than a nursing home.

Angelina reached across the table to rest her arms on top of Lucy's while she struggled to adjust to this shift in the universe, to make it make sense, to make it real, this world without Lucy. But she couldn't.

After she called 911 and turned off the heat, she moved her chair as close to Lucy as she could without moving the table so that Lucy was protected. She'd been wearing a t-shirt and sweatpants, eating a banana, and drinking the tea Angelina had brought her in the blue mug she'd also brought her. Sudden cardiac arrest, if Angelina had to guess. Maybe four or five hours ago—early this morning.

She hated that Lucy had been by herself. Why had John Milton left her? Maybe that's what killed Lucy. He couldn't have waited a little longer? Angelina stomped her foot.

She heard the ambulance. Why did they have to put the siren on? She'd told the dispatcher Lucy was dead, that she was a nurse, that she knew.

Angelina also knew she should call John Milton, but she wasn't going to leave Lucy's side. The siren was right outside now. Angelina could see the paramedics and the ambulance. But she didn't move.

A young guy came in first and fast, hopping from the cement block with a bag. Bright orange hair and lots of freckles.

"It's a mobile home," Angelina told him. "Not a trailer."

Another man and a woman appeared in the doorway. He held up a hand to them.

She knew he knew there was nothing to do.

"Are you the one who called?" the orange-haired guy asked.

Angelina nodded.

"You're her nurse?"

Angelina looked at Lucy. She stood, and with her hand on top of Lucy's head, she said, "I'm her friend."

And then she stepped out of the way.

●

Minutes later, a tall, out-of-breath woman with bright red lips appeared in the doorway.

"Oh, no," she said. "Is it Lucy?"

Angelina, who was standing in the kitchen, nodded. The paramedics were moving the table out of the way.

The woman rubbed her arms up and down, and she stepped into the kitchen so they could bring in the stretcher. Then she went right up to Lucy and gave her a hug.

"I've been afraid of this for years," the woman said, tearing up and moving back into the kitchen. "But I thought...You must be Angelina. I'm Gracie." And she hugged Angelina. "You were so good to her. She'd started getting out, and walking. Even over to visit with me. I thought maybe..." Gracie looked over at the paramedics who were trying to get Lucy out of the chair. "I heard the ambulance getting louder, then saw it slow down. Oh dear, I've got to get back to the store. I made everyone leave, but they're waiting and the door's unlocked." Gracie opened the drawer to the left of the sink and took out a scrap of paper and a pencil. "Here's my number," she said, leaning on the counter to write. "If I can do anything. And, you know, about the arrangements. I guess you already called John Milton."

Angelina nodded. She'd told the paramedics the same thing.

"Lucy gave him a big heart," Gracie said. "And it's going to break big."

Then the whirlwind in which she had arrived swooshed her out the door.

The paramedics were pressing Lucy onto the stretcher and shaking out a sheet to cover her. Angelina leaned against the kitchen counter to steady herself.

After they took Lucy away, Angelina propped a chair against the door to hold it closed. She eased the table and chairs back where they belonged. She scooped up Lucy's banana peel with the one bite left and threw it in the trash. After getting warm water going in the sink, she added some green Palmolive liquid and went back for Lucy's mug. Giving it to Lucy had been an afterthought—she'd bought it to support the hospital. Angelina cupped a hand and poured the cold remains of Lucy's tea right into her palm. Lucy had used milk. Angelina stared at the creamy liquid as it leaked out. She blew what was left into the soapy water, then she closed her fingers over the last drop or two. She submerged the mug, let go of it, and watched it pop up.

With a fresh cloth, she washed the bottom that read, "The Flower Mug by Madison (age 14) North Georgia Hospital." She washed the handle shaped like an S with the bigger-than-life-size butterfly on top. She washed the dark blue outside, the yellow polka dots, the raised pink flower that looked like a daisy. She washed half-inch by half-inch around the rim and into the creamy insides. She rinsed the mug in water and dried it with a fresh towel. She touched the inside of the flower, holding her finger there for a moment, and then she returned the mug to its place in the cabinet.

Angelina had never been beyond the bathroom in either mobile home. Lucy kept the doors shut. Now she went to the edge of the kitchen and peered down the hallway. Before she was even through the open door, she could see the watercolors.

They covered the wall space and the fronts of the cabinets and the closet door. Lots of green and purple. Flashes of white. The colors seemed faded, though, as if they'd disappeared into the paper. She wanted to go in after them.

Standing in front of the bed, Angelina looked in all directions. Each picture was some sort of little house, the ones on the wall by the bed all had a sloped roof, two front windows, one door, a black rocking chair, but the outside of each was a different light color—purple, yellow, and brown. Above Lucy's bed, the houses had flat roofs with a little boy in a red shirt on top, a bird on his arm, the houses all a deep blue and the different thing was the color of the bird—red, blue, and yellow. Three there too—in fact, turning around, each watercolor seemed part of a series of three. Above the pictures with the birds were cabinets that spanned the wall and came down each side turning into night tables, creating a recessed area for the bed to fit into—Lucy's giant arms.

The bed was rumpled, the white sheets with tiny purple and green flowers growing in all directions and a comforter to match. Angelina slipped out of her shoes and crawled in, inhaling Lucy and feeling her warmth. It did feel safe between the giant arms. As if all you needed to feel safe was to be tucked in and surrounded. No house was alone in Lucy's watercolor world. Each one belonged to two others.

Angelina went over to the 7-Eleven for some wire, a hammer, and nails. Gracie wouldn't let her pay. Standing on the cement block, with the sky washed-out and devoid of color, she hammered a nail into the frame and wrapped the wire around the doorknob and the nail. John Milton could deal with it later. Now it was time—past time—for her to deal with him. She got in the car, found his number in her file, and called without taking time to think of what she would say.

"Yep," he answered the phone.

"John Milton?"

"That's me."

"This is Angelina. Your mother's nurse."

He laughed. "I know who you are."

She smiled, and then her heart caught, like a piece of cloth on a nail. "I need to give you something. From your mother. Where are you?"

"Now? I could just swing by there after work."

"I need to give it to you now."

"I'm about thirty feet up in the air, out by the ramp to the interstate."

"I'm on my way."

●

As she got close to the interstate, she could see a billboard on the ground and a bunch of trucks and men who were standing around doing nothing. She pulled into the Dunkin' Donuts parking lot, which was as close as it looked like she could get, and that sad feeling she'd had when she was here after spending the night in her closet drifted over her again.

John Milton was leaning against the back of his truck, next to a bumper sticker she'd never noticed. *At least I can still smoke in my truck.* When she looked back at his face, he was shimmering in the weird way Nadine and Francis did, in that way that made Angelina want to figure out the secret. She wanted to say he commanded something, but that wasn't right. It was that he was commanding. She gathered her purse and got out of the car.

He was moving toward her, not like a bear but like a man—slow, strong steps, as if this were his place to defend. Maybe it was the boots. She no longer thought he resembled Lucy. His black hair and beard looked just as they had the first time she'd seen him four weeks ago, as if they were attempting to take off in all directions. He had on a long underwear shirt and a down vest. And jeans. He smiled at her, and her heart squeezed again.

He didn't know and she had to tell him, and a mother was a mother, which made this man a son. Lucy's boy. Angelina's chest heaved in a kind of dry sob, the closest she'd been to tears. As if she could only feel her own loss now that she could imagine his.

"What is it my mother had to give me that couldn't wait?"

He seemed even bigger and taller than when he'd cornered her by her car. "It's bad news, I'm afraid. Do you want to come sit in my car?"

His smile disappeared. His expression became focused. "Tell me," he said. "Straight up."

"Lucy died this morning, John. She was dead when I got there."

He jerked his hand to his back pocket as if she'd just told him his wallet was gone and he was checking to see if that could possibly be right. Then he reached for Angelina's shoulder, at the same time shoring himself up and keeping her at a distance. She wrapped her arm around his, feeling his muscles below the rough, dark hair on his arm.

"I stayed with her until the paramedics got there. Did you know her bedroom was covered with watercolors?"

"I shouldn't have left her," he said, looking as if he were going to crumble.

"Children are supposed to leave," she said—which she knew to be true and yet she agreed that John Milton should not have left

Lucy. "You were only doing what you were meant to do. Lucy knew that." And yet she wasn't sure Lucy *had* known that.

"I might have been able to help her," he said.

"The paramedics think it was quick. Her heart."

John Milton put his other hand to his heart.

"She was still sitting at the table. She hadn't tried to move."

John Milton turned to Angelina and, letting his outstretched arm collapse, he leaned down, reaching his giant arms around her before she could get her arms out to put around him. He swallowed her up, and it felt good. She let go and inhaled sweat and pine.

"It'll be okay," they said at the same time.

CHAPTER 37

Thirty minutes after arriving home to an empty garage and pouring half a bottle of lavender oil into a hot bath, she could hear Will shouting *Angelina* into the air as if he was worried she might not really be there.

The bathroom door opened. "Angelina?" He came all the way in, and now he could see her. "There you are."

"Lucy was dead when I got there this morning."

"Oh dear, I'm sorry. Heart attack?"

"Basically. Sudden cardiac arrest. Or that's what the paramedics thought."

"Is there anything I can get you?"

"I'll be down after a while."

"Take your time," he said.

At the click of the door, Angelina turned on the hot water and dumped in the rest of the bottle.

Even after a longer-than-usual bath, when she started down the stairs, the sun was still sending out brilliant streaks of orange although it had fallen low in the sky. In the kitchen, two glasses and the wine waited on the counter; Will waited at the table. She wished she wanted to sit on the porch with him.

"You go on," he said, jumping up and handing her a coat, which she put on. "I'll bring the wine."

Outside she sat in her rocker. That fast, only a few puddles of orange close to the horizon. The color was leaving this day, as if it had another life to run off to somewhere else. Angelina felt something bearing down on her. She stood and took off the coat.

"It's warmer than I thought," Will said. "Warmer than it was." He set her wine on the table and sat down in his rocker.

"How was your day?" she forced herself to ask.

"I drove out to the headwaters."

"The headwaters?"

"I made the right decision," he said.

She picked up her wine and sat down again, took a sip. "What do you mean?"

"I was glad not to be there for work," Will said, coughing. "We should go and take a picnic sometime."

Angelina exhaled and looked at the sweet man rocking beside her, knowing she couldn't be who he wanted her to anymore.

"Was it bad?" Will asked.

"Could have been worse," she said, searching for some trace of the sun. "She'd only been dead a few hours. I had to kick the door in."

"You kicked in the door?"

"Of a mobile home. It was aluminum."

"Still."

"And I had to tell her son."

"Was he okay?"

She nodded, slugging some wine without tasting it. "You know, I've seen people die before. And I've seen dead people before. I don't think I'll ever get used to it." She drained her glass. "Everything is so still."

Will stood and stretched.

The sun was gone, and she missed it.

He reached for her glass. "I'll get you some more."

"Do we have any tequila?" she asked.

"Tequila? I don't think so. We have Scotch."

She shook her head. "Just the wine then."

The door closed, and she looked out at the darkness that had fallen around her. She would be assigned a new patient next week, but she wasn't sure she wanted another one.

Will came back, handing her a full glass. "What's for dinner?"

"I have no idea," she said. "I don't care about food. And I'm tired of cooking."

He cleared his throat and moved to the screen, looking toward the mountains.

They didn't often need a light out here and hadn't turned one on tonight. Out past Will, the mountains stood as a solid darkness against a porous, dark sky.

"I'm tired of doing things I don't care about," she said. "Life is too short."

"I agree." He turned around to face her. "We're on the same side there."

"If you don't have to go to work," she said. "I don't have to cook supper."

He came over and sat beside her. "This is a fine mess we've gotten ourselves into."

She couldn't help but smile. His hand was resting on the arm of his rocker. She reached over and put hers on top of his, feeling the rough hairs and the bones, the ups and downs, the cold, smooth band he wore.

He squeezed her fingers and stood. "I'll go see what I can dig up for us to eat."

CHAPTER 38

At Union Cemetery, gray clouds raced across the sky, passing over the sun one by one, turning the world light and dark and light and dark. The wind swirled dead leaves and threads of pine straw. Angelina tightened the wool scarf around her neck and buttoned her top button against the cold air she usually welcomed. The bare branches bounced in the wind. It was much colder now at eleven than it had been at eight this morning.

Under the tent, John Milton stood at the front. On his right, an older woman with sunglasses on her head. Angelina wondered if she was a girlfriend. On his left, a man with his hands in the pockets of a too-small suit. Maybe his boss, the man who had spoken to her the other day before she left John Milton, but he'd had a haircut and a shave and stood now with an overweight woman. Gracie stood in front of Angelina, with her black-red hair hanging over the back of a red coat. A tall, lanky boy in a jean jacket, who looked as if he might be her son, stood next to her. Another man wearing a navy blazer was approaching with a woman on his arm.

Angelina put her arm through Will's. They'd been married twenty-three years. Good days followed bad days just as bad days followed good ones. And here, in the midst of how-short-life-could-be, she was glad she wasn't alone and glad he was the one standing next to her and glad they were together.

At 11:05, a man in a dark suit nodded to John Milton, who stepped forward by himself. His hair looked as if he'd tried to wet it down, but strands were snapping loose, either of their own accord or at the direction of the wind. He wore dark pants, a white shirt, a red tie. No jacket or coat. He put his hands by his side.

"I'd like to thank all of you for coming." He stepped back and rested his left palm on the casket. "The day Lucy died I cut a tree where I live. Then I made her this little house that smells of pine. Earlier this morning I put the top on."

As John Milton raised and again lowered his hand onto the lid of the casket, Will clutched at her arm.

"What is it?" she whispered.

He shook his head.

"The smell of pine I remember from growing up," John Milton said. He paused and then said, in an amazed, lighter voice, "Her bedroom was papered in watercolors."

She wondered if maybe he hadn't known.

He turned and put both hands on the coffin. After a minute, he faced the group again. "I put three of those watercolors on the underside of her roof in there. They belonged together, and they belonged with Lucy." He looked into the faces of each of the people there. When his eyes found Angelina's, he paused.

"My mother did everything for me. She loved me. I loved her." He turned and wrapped his arms around the coffin.

It was such a natural gesture that Angelina marveled she'd never seen anyone do it before. Leaning into Will, she held her breath.

John Milton kissed the top of the box and stepped back. The man in the suit nodded to another man in a long coat, who cranked the coffin into the ground.

No way could Angelina take another patient. She had not been firm enough about Lucy losing weight. She should have insisted. She should have knocked that candy out of Lucy's hands. She had to see the watercolors again.

She and Will were waiting to speak to John Milton when Gracie with her red lips approached, and again she thanked Angelina for all she'd done. The tall boy came up beside her.

"Angelina," Will said. "This is Clyde from the coffee shop."

Clyde nodded.

"Are you Clyde's mother?" Will asked, "the one who loves Jackson Browne?"

Gracie nodded. To Angelina, she said, "We make a little circle. I know you and you know Will and Will knows Clyde and Clyde knows me."

"Angel," Will said, "you and Gracie should talk about Jackson Browne sometime."

Gracie patted her on the arm. "We sure should."

"So," Angelina said. "The 7-Eleven *and* the little coffee shop?"

"Yep," Gracie said. "That awful convenience store and another one out by the interstate support my little dream shop."

Angelina had to get away from all this polite chatter, which made her feel as if she were disappearing. "Nice to meet you, Clyde," she said. "We need to speak to John Milton. He's all by himself."

Gracie looked in that direction and squeezed her arm. "We'll talk later. Nice to meet you, Will."

Angelina went right up to John Milton, and he leaned over and wrapped his arms around her, just like he'd done the other day after she'd told him. It was as if he'd caught her. Like she used to catch caterpillars that had found their way indoors. After she was sure she had them, she would let them inch their way over her hand and then she would release them in a safe spot outside. She inhaled pine. His body around hers did not make her feel claustrophobic or make it hard for her to breathe.

He raised his head first, then one arm loosened, but he kept his left arm around her.

She looked into his blue eyes, and said, "You made her box?"

He nodded.

"You put watercolors in there?"

"I did."

"That was perfect."

He stuck out his hand, and Angelina followed it to find Will standing there.

"I'm Will. Angelina's husband."

"Thanks for coming," John Milton said. "Lucy was always talking about Angelina."

"I'll be glad to help you with her things," she said.

"Gracie offered too," John Milton said.

"I'm sorry for your loss," Will said, stepping away.

CHAPTER 39

Will looked around to discover that he and Angelina were upstairs at the same time, something that rarely happened unless they were asleep. When he came out of the bathroom, she was wrapping herself in the silky throw blanket she kept at the foot of the bed.

"Why don't you just get a sweater?" he asked.

"I don't feel good," she said. "I'm really cold."

She pulled the covers down and slid in, still wrapped in the other blanket.

"You probably got chilled standing outside all that time."

She rolled over, pulling the covers above her ears.

"Can I get you anything?" he asked.

"Will you pull down the shades?"

He was having trouble getting the window closed after it had been open for so long.

"Leave the window open," she said.

"But you're cold?"

She didn't respond. He couldn't get it closed anyway. One by one, he pulled on white cords, lowering the three blackout shades they never used. Each layer of darkness seemed to put more distance between them. He glanced at her oblong shape under the blankets in a room that felt as if it were growing thick.

Heading downstairs Will worried about Angelina. As if she might be on the verge of a breakdown. Something had happened with Lucy's son. It could be sexual, but he didn't think so. And how in the world had he not been able to see what he was doing with the boxes until Lucy lay dead in one that John Milton had made. The same John Milton who had wrapped his arms around his wife in a too-familiar way.

Periodically, Will got up from his chair and the TV to check on Angelina, sometimes just opening the door to confirm she was still there. Sometimes he stood for a minute and listened into the darkness for her breath. Sometimes he replaced her empty glass with fresh water. He felt her head as she had done for the children when they were little, but he didn't know if she had fever or not.

His concern seemed too personal to bother the girls about. In fact, it seemed like something he should protect them from. He knew bad things happened in the world, but he hadn't thought they would ever happen to their family. But that's what everyone must think until the bad thing happened.

He had counted on Angelina, and now he wondered if that had been a mistake.

Then his worry began to change shape, and he stopped checking on her. "I have a heart too," he said to the empty hallway.

When Lucy's son had hugged her, it was like she disappeared. She was there. Then she wasn't. Then she was back again, only altered. Only sick.

Dusk came and went, the porch forgotten and ignored. Darkness spilled down the stairs and into the rest of the house. Will wandered through empty rooms. In the dining room, he couldn't bear to look out the windows at the world of cars and trash bins. He picked up a coaster with a tarnished silver rim.

Quickly and quietly, he replaced it on the sideboard exactly as it had been. He had come home. Was it her turn to be out in the world now? He'd never imagined that. They had three daughters. They were a hub. Thanksgiving and then Christmas.

He slept on the sofa in the den. In the morning, he could see she'd been in the kitchen. The orange juice was on the counter. He picked it up—half full and warm. She'd just left it sitting out. He tiptoed up the stairs and cracked the door. She was back in her darkened room, her rumpled bed. He closed the door quietly. This was bigger than Lucy.

Back in the kitchen, he made coffee. Then he banged a mug on the counter, cracking it. He hurled it into the trash and chose another. His hands shook as his eyes followed the black liquid from the glass pot to a stainless-steel mug.

She'd hardly mentioned the son, and then there he was. Wrapping his arms around her.

And without even asking.

Halfway to the basement door, he stopped. He couldn't face the boxes. He turned toward the porch. He couldn't go out there either. So he stood in the hallway, like an idiot as Angelina would say, and drank his coffee.

Over the next few days, they existed separately—he moving during the day, she apparently during the night, leaving saltines or juice on the counter like clues. Friday, Saturday, Sunday wiped off the map. He didn't go into their bedroom for clean clothes or through the bedroom to the bathroom for his toothbrush. The phone didn't ring. Not once. Not even a wrong number. Why did they even have it?

He stood by the front door, his hands in his pockets. He stood by the back door. He didn't dare leave the house. For fear. For fear of what? That she wouldn't be here when he got back? He hated himself. He wondered if she had the flu, if she were depressed, if she were taking pills. He was afraid to go into their room, to sit on their bed, to put his hand on her leg. He was afraid to ask her if he could do anything. He was afraid to push her—for fear of the direction she might take.

On Monday morning, he sat at the kitchen table with a cup of coffee and without a placemat, in the same clothes he'd worn since Friday. For the first time in his life, he understood Angelina's mother, understood how you could be afraid of being afraid, and how the only place you had a chance of being safe was home. Looking at the back door and the windows, he got up. He turned out the kitchen light and pulled down the shade over the small window on the door. He double-checked the lock. One by one, he closed the shutters he'd never seen shut. In the dining room, when he tried to draw the curtains, he was astonished to find they didn't move. The front door. He fought the urge to move the sideboard in front of it. Instead, *he* leaned against it, and then he slid to the floor, where he lay, his hands pillowing his head, his knees tucked to protect his body.

He awoke to find the sun burnished to a color that felt less invasive. Still, he closed the curtains in the den he'd neglected to close earlier in the day. He peed and drank three glasses of water, feeling as if he should be sticking a hunting knife into the waist of his pants. With the imaginary knife as courage, he climbed the stairs, his head heavy and muddled, and he turned the knob quietly, entering their room, which smelled rancid, as if she'd been throwing up. After his eyes adjusted, he went to the bed, where she still lay, unmoving in a tangle of sheets, no evidence of vomit. He felt her head—clammy. No fever, he guessed. She didn't stir at his touch, which meant she was awake. He left the room.

On the bottom step, he felt faint and grabbed the rail. He checked his own head for fever, and it felt like fire, but he made it to the door, sliding again to resume his vigil at its feet, giving in to the coming of night and the contagion of sleep.

A car door slammed, and his eyes popped open to bright morning light. His body prickled with alertness. He was drenched in sweat. The doorbell. *Jesus, Mary, and Joseph,* he clutched his heart. He sat up, feeling the presence of another person just behind him. The doorbell rang again, and Will struggled to his feet. He brushed his hair into place with his fingers as he looked through the peephole.

Damnation. The bug man. He leaned a shoulder against the door. But when the bell rang a third time, he unlocked it and jerked it open.

Rick stepped a foot and swung a canister across the threshold, shoving a stack of newspapers toward Will. "Hey, my man, I was beginning to think nobody was home."

Will dropped the papers on the floor and anchored his body in front of Rick.

"Look out there, buddy," Rick said.

"You can't come in."

Rick's bicep was still bulging from his sleeve.

Rick looked at him, raising an eyebrow. "It's Tuesday."

"It may very well be," Will said, tucking in his shirt and standing up straight, feeling stronger.

"It's on my schedule."

"I don't care if you have orders from the Pope," Will said, taking a step forward, "you're not coming in today."

"I don't understand."

"It's simple. This is my house, goddammit. And you're not coming in." And with that, Will pushed Rick back to the other side of the threshold and slammed the door. Then he locked it and marched to the bathroom. He peed, threw water on his face, and gargled. He couldn't remember the last time he'd brushed his teeth.

He headed up the steps without attempting to be quiet. He knew she was awake; at the very least, she would have heard the doorbell. He opened the bedroom door, leaving it open; he went through the darkness to the bathroom and started the shower. Then he turned to the tub, started the bathwater, and added in some Rosemary Bath Oil that changed the water from clear to red. He took off all his clothes, leaving them in a pile on the floor instead of putting them in the hamper.

Letting the water continue to run in the tub, he stepped into the shower. The hot water rid his body of sweat and any remaining beads of uncertainty. He tilted his head up and breathed out.

Minutes later, he emerged and toweled off, starting at his head and addressing every area of his body down to his toes. The way he dried off drove Angelina crazy. *Angelina.*

He checked the temperature of the bath, turned off the hot water, and let the cold run for a second longer. He stood and faced the bedroom. Then he wrapped the towel around his waist and advanced—resisting the urge to throw back the covers in grand fashion as if this were the wild west and he had come to claim his woman. Instead he sat on the edge of the bed.

She lay on her side, facing in, away from where he sat, the extra blanket she'd wrapped herself in on Thursday abandoned on his side of the bed. He sat closer and fingered strands of hair out of her face.

She was the love of his life. But she wanted an empty house and he wanted *to be in the house* with her—with her wanting to be here with him. And he couldn't make her want that.

Opening the drawer of her bedside table, he searched for the scissors he knew were there. He stood and moved the covers off her feet. He held the bottom of her pajama pants between the blades of the scissors, having to move the thin yellow fabric twice before the blade caught. He cut, each cut searing him as if he were cutting his own fingers. He moved the covers out of the way as he went, listening to her breathing. It was slow going, as he imagined it would be to remove barbed wire from an injured animal. He cut all the way up to the waistband, and with extra force, there it went. He wiped sweat from his forehead and started with the sleeve of the arm on top and then he leaned over her and cut her shirt up the middle. The bottom fell open, baring her left breast. He took a breath and put the scissors on the table. He stood over her, surprised she still had not moved, and he peeled her clothes off, amazed at the beauty of this body he had loved for so many years and through so much. He touched the puckered flesh of her arm, rolling her onto her back. Her eyes were open. Which startled him so that he paused for a moment. Then he slid the other sleeve off and the other pajama leg. He couldn't help reaching for her, placing his hands palm down on her stomach. She closed her eyes. He left his hands a minute longer, feeling the gurgling beneath, the pulsing of blood. When he took his hands away, she opened her eyes and looked into his, and he leaned over and put his face on her stomach where his hands had been. He inhaled the mustiness of her skin, and he opened his mouth, so hungry for her he didn't think he could stand it. He straightened and scooped her into his arms, and the first move she made in all of this was to lean her head against his shoulder. As he rounded the corner toward the bathroom, his towel fell off. He kept going—a naked fifty-three-year-old husband carrying his naked forty-nine-year-old wife. It was a picture he had never had in his head until this moment and yet here it was and he was responsible for it.

By the tub, Will bent his knees and squatted until he felt the side, and then he leaned over to place Angelina in the scented red water. He wanted to lie down on top of her. But on his knees, he wet the washrag and wrung it out. He pulled her hair back and wiped her forehead, her eyes, her nose and cheeks. Her mouth. He clutched the soap, wet it, and lathered her neck, her breasts, her stomach. Below the bubbles and into the red water, he dropped the soap and kept going by feel. Unable to stifle a small moan, he bit his lip. *This is for her, dammit.*

He found the soap and continued down each leg. He threaded his fingers between her toes, then he grabbed all five for a second, finding her toe that was different, longer than the others, squeezing all of them as hard as he dared. He rinsed her off, let the rag fall to the bottom of the tub, and stood before her, feeling comfortable and himself in a way he hadn't even realized he'd no longer been feeling. Then he left the bathroom, shutting the door he wanted to leave open.

CHAPTER 40

The man who'd cut her out of her pajamas was the man she'd fallen in love with a quarter century ago. The cutting loose was a gift to her, she knew. And she smiled—he could still flip her insides. Leaning up in the tub, making waves, she opened the drain. Then she turned on the water and stuck her head underneath.

Before going downstairs, she added the strawberry lip gloss that Iris had told her would help her dry lips. In the bedroom, when she opened the shades, there, in a pile by the bed, were the remains of the yellow pajamas Will had given her for her birthday.

Downstairs, Will had made coffee, and she poured herself a cup. Her stomach, as empty as she could ever remember it being, heaved at the dark acid. She put the cup in the sink and instead, ran water in a glass. On the way to join Will on the porch, where she knew, without looking, he would be, she collected her jacket. They never came out here in the morning anymore, and she was surprised at how moist and white the air was, at how they seemed to be wrapped in fog. Angelina waved her arm through it, then sat in her rocker, putting her glass on the table that had lasted as long as they had.

"So," she said.

"Yep," he said.

Her resentment was gone. She didn't feel as if she had to be on guard anymore and breathed in the cool air. "I love you, you know."

"I know," he said, rocking back and forth. "But sometimes it doesn't feel like you do."

His head was leaning against the back of his chair. She rose and touched the screen, feeling as if she were touching the mountains themselves. "I don't know why I didn't tell you how much I was counting on the empty house, on having time to myself again."

"I wanted to stop working," he said. "I wanted to be at home and to spend more time with you. I don't know why I didn't tell you that."

Birds sang around them, landing on trees, taking off, returning, and sunlight fell across her glass of water on the table, illuminating a path.

CHAPTER 41

Nine days after the funeral, Angelina drove to Lucy's hoping to find John Milton, but all she found was cold hard earth. As if the last six weeks had never happened. She pulled in over the curb and pulled to a stop in the middle of all the empty space. Then she turned off the car, leaned back, and closed her eyes. Despite being enclosed in her car and despite the overcast day and the barren surroundings, she felt some kind of energy, a tingling that proved yes, something *had* happened.

At the 7-Eleven, before the door shut behind her, Gracie said, "He bought some land, out off Old Highway 7. I have the directions."

"You knew I'd be back?"

"And it didn't take any kind of superpowers."

Angelina smiled.

"He was here all last weekend—just hanging around and replacing the door. I saw him drive by and went over to help him pack up Lucy's clothes for the shelter. I cleaned up but he said cleaning didn't make me shine like it had Lucy. You did a number on that door. He even had to replace the hinges."

"Stronger than I know."

"Aren't we all, sister?"

Angelina pulled off the highway onto a newly cleared dirt road. The trailers sat off to the left. John Milton stood on a rise behind them, and it looked as if he were watching her drive in. So she drove slowly and parked behind his red truck. By the time she got out of the car, he was no longer watching; he was digging. And Lady was running around barking.

Before climbing up to see him, she went over to the trailers and turned in all directions. A triangle. As if wagons had gathered around a fire at the end of the day. And Lucy's trailer had a new purple door. Angelina stood in front of it and looked out, feeling the giant arms of the other two trailers. Above, the faraway sky and sun. The slight wind. She felt proud of John Milton and happy for Lucy. This was just as it should be.

Angelina climbed the small hill.

A pile of old boards lay off to the left, along with four old telephone poles. John Milton had dug three holes and the fourth was in the works. He watched her move toward him.

"Lucy would have liked it," she said.

"If Lucy was in that trailer, it wouldn't be here."

"Mobile home," she said, only remembering up against someone else.

"Lucy only called it a mobile home when she was upset or talking about Catfish. The rest of the time, they were trailers."

She looked down at her car, over to the mobile homes, and back to John Milton.

"I had to move away," he said. "Having my own trailer was not enough. Lucy was always in it."

"You have a nice piece of land," she said.

He stopped digging and smiled. "And, if you can believe this, a train too. Goes through the trees on the southeast corner." He pointed.

Angelina glanced in that direction.

John Milton scooped out one more pile of dirt then threw down the shovel. He picked up a sack and poured powder in an old rusted red wheelbarrow. He added water from a bucket and stirred.

"Cement?" she asked.

He nodded, lifting the back end of the wheelbarrow and rolling it over to the holes. She stayed where she was. He tipped some cement into the first hole, retrieved one of the poles, and heaved it into the cement. He stood there holding it and looking at her.

"Do you need any help?" she asked.

"Does it look like I need help?"

"I was just trying to be nice."

"Why don't you try being you?"

She turned away, feeling her face heat up. "This is a good spot to build," she said, "You'll have an amazing view."

"The sky putting on a show every day." He looked up. "Rain coming. Hard to get anything done in November."

But she didn't look up; she looked over at him.

He looked back at her. "I bet you feel like a cloud. I mean, the way a cloud would feel if I could get my arms around a cloud."

She tried not to look away, but it was too much.

"When I first heard your voice, when you called about Lucy, I thought ping, surely no flesh attached itself to such disheartened sounds. Your voice made me think of yellow, of a baby chick without its mother."

She felt pressure on her chest.

"Every time I see you," he said, "you seem lighter, like one day you might just fly away. And yellow, there's still something yellow about you."

"I'm a coward."

"It's a different yellow. A soft, starting-out kind of yellow. Pale, uncertain."

Whatever this was, she couldn't do it. "What are you going to do with the trailers?"

He let go of the pole and took a few steps. "Maybe build a fire pit in the middle. Get a folding chair."

She turned to face him. "Did you know about the watercolors?"

He started on the second pole. "I hadn't been in her bedroom since I moved her furniture in there."

"Could I look at them again?"

"The door's unlocked," he said.

She started down the hill.

"You know..." he said.

She stopped but did not turn around.

"If you were a yo-yo on a string, I'd snap you back this instant."

She picked up momentum from the slope of the earth, but even though she was heading away, it felt as if she were running straight toward him. She looked up. The wind was stronger now, and the trees were leaning, the clouds darker, racing across the sky, crashing into each other.

CHAPTER 42

Angelina opened Lucy's new purple door, not bothering to close
it. In the bedroom, instead of looking at the watercolors that
were still there, which was what she came to do, she stared at the
large bare area above the bed where the three watercolors used
to be, the ones that were now deep in the earth. She imagined
Lucy running her fingers along the edge of the wood, inhaling
that pine scent, smiling at the little boy in the red shirt standing
high on the roof of the house.

She slipped out of her shoes and lay down on top of the flowery
comforter that, as she got closer, still smelled of Lucy.

Now Angelina was cozy in the space Lucy had left and
wondered if she herself would leave. A question she could never
have anticipated three months ago. And three weeks ago, she
couldn't voice, even to herself.

Despite all her sleeping, all her letting go, she felt herself falling
again into sleep.

●

A rough kiss bam on her lips, and she opened her eyes, not startled or scared. She touched his soft lips with her finger, as if she
were drawing, then she touched her own. But looking up at a

man other than Will and it being what she wanted was too much. Too much. She swiveled away, off the bed, out of the room, and was thankful to be drenched in stormy weather.

CHAPTER 43

This, Will decreed, *was the morning he needed to hear the wind sing.* The Corinthian Bells, as they were called, hand-tuned to G, had arrived the week before in a long rectangular cardboard box. Wind chimes were something Will had wanted for eons. He unwrapped the three aluminum alloy tubes that would not rust, that hung from a circular top. It took him only an hour to affix them to the side of the house between the grill and the porch, which was where he stood again now. He'd done his part and was waiting. He knew there could be value in waiting, even if it was for something as unpredictable as the wind. Then he thought, perhaps the wind was like a watched pot.

Inside, he paced up and down the hall. Since Lucy's funeral, he'd been unable to go to his workroom, unable to face the boxes. He had avoided and avoided.

And now he was going to avoid some more. He got in his car and drove to Running on Empty. For the first time, Gracie was there, with her big red lips and weird-colored hair. After the funeral, and what with all the connections, he felt as if he knew her. Of course she wasn't Stella, but she was right here in front of him. "Take It Easy" was playing in the background. Will bought Gracie a latte and asked questions for as long as he could think of them—her husband killed in a car accident right after they got married, right after she'd told him she was pregnant; Clyde living at home now looking for a job; Lucy's perfect, empty trailer. When Will opened the door to leave, as Jackson Browne's voice sang overhead "*And the river opens for the righteous,*" which never failed to make him smile, he saw Clyde getting out of a beat-up car.

"Hey, Clyde, I tried a latte today."

Clyde just smiled and kept going. So Will did too.

On his return home, approaching the garage, he felt himself braking instead of forging ahead. Had he learned nothing? He jerked himself out of the car, thrust his key in the back door, slammed the door behind him, stormed to the basement, grabbed the brass knob, and turned.

CHAPTER 44

On her second visit to John Milton, she got out of the car, glanced once at the structure he was building, and then kept her eyes on him, watching as he looped his hammer into his work belt, as he took a step down off the ladder, as he rested against the ladder to watch her approach. She pulled her black jacket close around her.

"Angelina, Angelina," he said.

"Hey, yourself," she said, stopping about three feet away from him.

"That's a colorful scarf," he said. "For you."

She nodded at the wooden structure. "That's an odd house for you."

"You think I'm building a house?"

"I just thought…" She glanced at the trailers and breathed out. "I guess I assumed you'd want a real house. I don't know why. It makes no sense."

"Billboard," he said.

She took several steps back and then sat on the ground facing the structure, which in her defense could have been the side of a house if the house were going to be up off the ground. She could see now that of course it was more like a billboard. There was a wooden ledge at the bottom of the frame, built across the four poles he'd been putting in the ground the last time she was here. He'd filled in the frame with boards—six of them. About halfway up the pole on the right end, there was something like a ladder.

"Hand-painted signs by me," he said.

"But nobody will see them."

"I will."

She watched his billboard as if it might take off before she could take it all in.

He came to sit beside her, then he lay back on the cold ground. "Whenever I'm this close to it, I generally go all the way down. I like to visit with the grass, the millions and millions of blades." He yanked one and put it in his mouth. "Tart green. And pine, can you smell the pine in the air? I've always wished air had a color."

Angelina lay on her back too, brushing his arm, not knowing if she'd done it on purpose.

"The air smells just like it did when Lucy used to clean all the time. I don't remember the offices—just the smell of pine. The trashcans were full of paper, what with no recycling, and she would pick out the pieces that weren't wet with coffee and stack them up real neat. I remember the stacking—the thwump thwump on the table. Lucy didn't like cleaning offices. She said the black and white and angles made her feel empty. So when she thought she'd saved enough paper for forever, she switched to houses. I remember those."

"I miss Lucy," she said.

"I've been looking for my own piece of land for a long time, ever since I felt the slickness of the first computer-generated vinyl billboards. It was cool to see a design I'd created on the computer arrive giant-sized in a box, but I had to force my brain to connect what I had "drawn" on a screen to that slickness. I knew I was going to need wide open spaces—enough space so that I could build, so I could still feel my hand move and see something real appear."

"How did you get started doing billboards?"

"It's a long story. Lucy always wanted to hear it all."

"I want to hear it all too."

"I was in high school, and the March before graduation a sign appeared in the drugstore window. Red, magic-markered words on shirt backing: *Sign Painter Wanted. Inquire at North Georgia Billboards. State Street.* I went on over and drew a sign for Cody—well, he was Mr. Calhoun then—on the back of my Algebra homework. I started to work the next day—two hours after school. Full time after graduation. The three of us and Patti." John Milton turned to her. "This is where Lucy always says, 'Patti?' Like she can't remember her."

"Patti?" Angelina said.

"Patti was twenty-three. And she taught me I liked older women better, the same way I liked crayons better after the points were softened up, after they were bits and pieces. Patti always said she called a spoon a spoon, but she called me "Mr. Big and Burly," which I liked because of the *b*'s, but Patti said it was because I was hard on the outside and soft on the inside. I told her that sounded like an egg."

Also like a candy bar, Angelina thought.

John Milton turned on his side to face her. "This is where Lucy always says it sounds like a candy bar to her."

Angelina grabbed his arm and turned on her side.

He closed his eyes for a minute. "The first time I stood in the large warehouse with the gigantic frame of the board in front of me, it was hard to breathe. I wanted the job, but I also wanted my index card or a piece of notebook paper. I felt big and small at the same time. But Mr. Calhoun brought in an overhead projector like we had at school. Turned out I was supposed to draw just like always, then they put the drawing on the glass and beamed a quarter of it at a time to the paper. All I had to do was copy the lines that were there. Then paint. The four pieces got pasted together up on the board. Mr. Peters explained how deep I would have to pound a post into the ground for a structure, how to pull the ladder down, how to take the sections up in a bag, to white out the old ad before affixing the new one, but if too many were on top of each other, to scrape off the old ones. I was shaking my head the whole time he was talking. I told him, 'I'm a sign painter and I work alone.' He rested his hands on the tailgate of his truck and said, 'John Milton, your specialty is painting the signs. Cody's specialty is selling the signs. Mine is getting the structures up. Patti is the glue that holds us all together. The four of us, we're a team.'"

John Milton placed his hand flat on the grass between them. "I was born to paint signs," he said. "But it turned out I also liked to pound poles into the ground. And most of all, I loved to be high above the regular world—something I never would have discovered if I hadn't been forced to climb up the first time, which turned out to be just like the first plop of a skipping stone."

Angelina could see it all.

"So that was the story Lucy wanted to hear all the time. But there's more I could never tell her."

"Tell me."

"It turned out I never could paint the signs fast enough. I didn't know how to rush. As we got more business, I got more behind. I went from painting on sections of paper and putting up a face with a glue machine and a squeegee on a pole to painting on panels that were hoisted by cranes. Then like I said, that large square box arrived at the shop, and inside was a sample of a computer-generated vinyl face—a billboard all in one piece. I felt sick in my stomach. For a long time, vinyls cost too much for our small company, but eventually not. As I used the computer more and more, it felt like my signs were disintegrating. On a warm day in December, Cody told me I was painting my last one. From then on, I would only be using the computer."

He rolled onto his back. "That day, I saw how things split off from each other in a natural way. Like the tree trunk behind the Dairy Queen that Cody showed me when I was still in high school, using the word *bifurcate*. That's what my sign painting was doing—work going the speedy cool way and heart going some other way. *Bifurcate* is a word I like. Actually, I like to go one way with everything else going another. Until that day I had had no plan for my life. Nothing to work *for*. I told Lucy vinyls were taking over and I would be making less money. I gave her less money. Then I got a raise I didn't mention. Turned out I was just as good a sign painter on the computer as in real life."

She sat up, eyeing the structure. "It's like you've framed the woods. It's like," but she stopped. "It's weird. My eyes keep wanting to focus on one of the small rectangles where I can see through to the woods, but I can only see a small part of the woods." She felt like she was trying to piece something together.

He rolled to his side again, facing her. "I want to crash my face into your hair."

She breathed out, trying to be here now. But she couldn't look at him. A squirrel ran by in front of them. She tilted her head up. "The sky is so blue."

"But I never use the crayon named sky blue. I just use blue. And even then it's not right. Still, you'd think they would have matched the one blue crayon to the sky. There's so much of it and it's everywhere."

"I'd like to look at Lucy's watercolors again."

He sat up, brushing the edge of him against the edge of her.

"Every morning just before dawn," he said, staring up at the wide-open blue, "I climb to the top of a billboard with a thermos of coffee. I watch darkness change to light and night turn into day. I'm there when it happens. When the big picture reveals itself. That moment."

It was too much. With her finger, she reached to his mouth to stop the words, but midway her finger changed its mind and traced his stubby lips. Then she stood, brushed off her coat, and floated down the hill. When she looked back, he was still lying on the ground facing the billboard, but while she was watching him, he rolled onto his stomach and looked at her.

Again she stepped through the purple door.

CHAPTER 45

When Angelina opened Lucy's door, she felt oddly distant, and she'd expected to feel more comfortable. She sat at the table, sticking her hands in her coat pockets. Her whole body felt hot, and she slipped out of her coat, letting the arms hang limp off each side of the chair. Then she collected her coat and started down the hall, afraid the small rectangles of color might have lost their magic since the last time she was here.

Inside Lucy's room, her boots thudded across the linoleum to the three vertical rectangles taped to the closet door, each one the same three-storied treehouse. In the top one, the yellow sun was rising from the right corner; in the middle one, it was dead center overhead; in the bottom one, the sun was setting in the left corner.

She wanted to dive into the paintings, into oceans leading to other worlds, other lives. She wanted to go in after something, but what?

Inside the closet, it was empty except for an old shoebox on the floor, and she bent to open the top. Inside, hundreds of index cards. The little signs Lucy had told her about. Some were child-like, some skillfully detailed. All colors, one color, black and white, lots of red. Heads, hands, feet, toes, and fingers. Pig tails and dog ears. Baby chicks, tree branches, parts of tables, parts of chairs, glimpses of skies. The rays of the rising sun. Some with writing. *For Mama* on so many.

She felt pressure on her heart followed by relief. As if more space had been created, and she could breathe easier. She replaced the top and stood. She threw her coat on the bed and peeled off her boots. In front of the window, looking out at the empty trailer, again she imagined what it might be like to live by herself as Lucy had, and she shivered. She wondered if up against different people we become different people.

She'd eaten Lucy's candy. She'd sat in Lucy's chairs. She'd slept in Lucy's bed.

Lucy's bed—she backed up and sat down on it, looking back and forth from the paintings on the closet door to the window framing the empty trailer. Then she stood and inserted herself into that space between—the corner where the two walls came together—so that she could see neither the trailer nor the paintings, at which point she turned her back to the wall, pressing herself until she molded her body to the right angle; then she slid to the floor, crossed her legs, and rested, her hands palm up—open—even though that position had never worked for her in her life.

She shook her hair out in front of her.

She tried being still again, tried to feel the line running through her body—like the line running down the wall behind her. She thought she felt it and looked down, feeling a lovely, light emptiness in her hands—the weightlessness of her hands filled with nothing.

He was there at the door, and then he was squatting in front of her. He tried to cross his legs as she had but to no avail and ended by splaying them out in a V around her, close, their legs touching. He turned his palms toward the sky.

They sat still like that for how long she didn't know. He let go of a small one without moving. She said, "You know what I like most about you?"

"Everything?"

"Nothing separates your insides from your outsides. There's no filter. You are who you are."

"Who are you?" he asked.

"You seem grounded."

"I am not. I've always had my head in the clouds. And that's where I want to keep it."

Now Angelina looked into his eyes for something in particular. "You seem different than you used to be," she said.

"Things are always changing," he said, glancing out the window. "It's the way of the world. But maybe you're the one who's different."

Angelina waved her arms toward the walls. "Lucy made you who you are."

"And I loved her. But we shouldn't have been living together. I should have moved away ages ago." He leaned back on his hands. "I feel good knowing no one else is around. I like knowing this space is mine and that I inhabit it alone, that I can be in relation to no one."

"I'm here," she said.

"Temporarily."

She was snug in the corner and he was leaning back, away from her—and yet they were headed straight for each other.

He lifted his hand, held it suspended in the air for a second, and then he sat up and touched her right arm. "East," he said. He touched her left arm. "West." He touched the top of her head.

"North." Then he touched her where she wanted him to touch her and said, "South," letting his fingers linger and trail away. She closed her eyes.

"Patti from work," he said, "she's from California and her mother was part Wintu. That East-West thing is a Native American story. They don't use left and right for their bodies. Just the four points of the compass. As Patti says, the self is never lost." He burped. "Instead of telling me she wants to have sex, Patti tells me the whole East-West story."

Angelina knocked her head against the wall.

"Of course I want to have sex with you," he said. "That's what people do. But I also thought you'd like the story."

She said, "I'll never lose my bearings."

"According to Patti."

She resumed her position—sitting straight, her palms upturned, still.

"I met your husband," he said. "Why are you here?"

"I want something else."

"You don't love your husband?"

"That's the problem," she said. "I do."

"So you love him but..." John Milton said.

"Life's too short and I've had this one too long."

He raised up onto his knees, and his soft lips swept across her chapped ones. He leaned back. He hadn't touched her anywhere else. Then he leaned in again, this time his tongue tracing a circle around her mouth. When he leaned back again, his unfamiliar hands had moved to his thighs.

"I haven't broken the rules since I was fourteen years old," she said, tasting the strawberry on her lips.

"How will you know what's out there if you stay inside the lines?"

"But I don't know how to get outside," she said.

And he rocked forward and scooped her away from the safety of the walls and into his unsafe arms. He kissed her neck—from ear to ear. And when he looked into her eyes, she pulled his head to hers.

Afterwards, they lay naked on the floor and used their fingers to trace the mountains and valleys of their bodies.

"I feel like these watercolors have something to tell us," she said. "Like a dream."

"I'm glad she showed them to you."

Angelina shook her head. "She didn't."

"But the other day, you said you wanted to see them again."

"I saw them…after," she said.

"I have everything I want," he said.

"I want a place without rules," she said, pushing against the wall with her foot. "A place where I can move without hitting anything." She turned and brushed her finger across his face.

He closed his eyes.

"I know, I'm selfish."

He opened his eyes. "The self is selfish for a reason."

She sat up. "I need to see beyond my little world to the big one out there."

He turned her hand over and pressed his finger between her thumb and forefinger. She closed her eyes. His finger began to move across her palm, a pressure and a lightness at the same time, and when he reached the other side, his finger slid off the edge, and she opened her eyes.

CHAPTER 46

"Damn it, damn it, damn it," Will said to himself, his eyes going straight to the rows of boxes on the top two shelves. One at a time, he slapped his right hand down on a box, grasping top and bottom at the same time and moving it as a whole to his work-table. His left arm hung as if he'd unattached it.

After making seven and despite not wanting to make anymore, now he had nine. Nine little houses.

Of course Stella wasn't at Best Buy when he went back the last time. He'd placed her hair band in a box and squished the life right out of her.

His left side wanted to grab the hammer and smash each box to bits.

His right side wanted to sit with the boxes, to get to know them, to become comfortable with them.

The boxes—

He plopped down in his chair so hard that it rolled backwards.

That's who he was.

And then he stood. That's how he would hold this family together—he would be the box.

He'd provided for the family with money; now he would provide for it with heart. He would be the center. After all, he was apparently the only one who wanted to be here. So he *would* be here. He'd be here when the others wanted to come home. And then he'd be here to send them off again. He didn't have to smash the houses. He would be the house.

He made a guess, reached for a box, took off the lid, and turned it upside down over the trash. The silvery pink hair band fell out. He fisted his chest in a gentle manner. Heart. He would learn to be comfortable with the emptiness around him. Because this house was what he, Will Brooks, wanted—for himself, and for the others.

As he removed the lid from each box, he felt the chains swirl up, shake loose, and disappear, like birds into the distance.

CHAPTER 47

Angelina pulled into a service station on Route 7 and parked at the edge, where she could pull right out again. She had messed up big time. How could she go home? She knew what Kate's response would be. *The same way you always do.* And Angelina would say, *But things are different now,* her voice sounding too high and tinny, her stomach jumping around. And Kate would say, *Nothing is different at home.*

Angelina leaned her head against the steering wheel. She breathed in and breathed out—even breaths.

She raised her head. What would Lucy say?

You set off like a woman in a dream. Good for you.

And Lucy would wrap her arms around herself, and Angelina did.

She felt different, stronger. As if she had more choices now. But how would she park in their garage and walk through the back door?

A red Volkswagen bug pulled up. A young girl in a short yellow dress got out and went inside, and a second later, emerged holding hands with a mechanic. They skirted the side of the building and disappeared into the back. Then yellow flashed from the corner as overalls fell to the ground.

She started the car. Was she going to see people having sex everywhere now?

As she pulled back onto the highway, gravel caught under her tires and she instinctively lifted her foot off the accelerator. A mile or two later, she turned on the radio. *It was only sex*, she told herself. *A little exercise. Just a cigarette break*, she imagined the mechanic saying. *Then you walk back into the shop and fix the next carburetor.*

CHAPTER 48

Rocking on the porch, Angelina held onto her wine glass as if that was all that was keeping her tethered to earth. She forced herself to sip slowly. From time to time, one of them commented on the sound or the beauty of the chimes hanging off to the left.

"We're almost to our first real Thanksgiving," Will said. "The first one where all the girls have been gone so that it will be a real homecoming."

"I still think it's a mistake to force Livie to come home," she said, feeling the dampness of her hair. "She's too old for that."

"Actually, I called her yesterday and told her she could stay."

"You did?"

Will nodded.

She stopped rocking to look at him. "But Thanksgiving's just a week away."

"It wasn't too late. She said she'd think about it."

The chimes rang out—three notes. No, it wasn't too late. She relaxed back into her rocker. The wine glass felt loose in her hand. Her shoulders let go. The end of the day on the porch with Will, the beauty of the mountains in the distance. She smiled to herself in the dark, feeling more at home than she had in a long time, being here at this moment more like something she had

243

chosen than something she was required to do. She went back to rocking, glad she didn't have to be still.

"But I think she'll come," Will said. "I mean, she already has the ticket. And the return."

It was getting colder, the wind picking up, the chimes sounding more often, activity in the trees. It was completely dark now, earlier than normal.

"It feels like it might storm," she said.

"There's a big one heading our way. I'm surprised it hasn't already started."

Angelina closed her eyes for a minute to feel the wind rushing through her, but instead of feeling the wind she saw great oceans, small pieces of land, and bridges—bridges expanding and contracting. And she thought perhaps marriage should have expansion joints too, so that it could expand at times and contract at others, without causing faults in the structure itself. "I'm going to get another glass of wine," she said. "And some chips."

"Chips now? Right before dinner?"

She smiled and stood, listening to the rocking chair rocking even without her. That was Will—no chips before dinner—and she loved him to pieces. As she went by, she touched his shoulder. "Do you need anything?"

"I'm good," he said.

"I'll be back," she said.

CHAPTER 49

Later, with Will snoring beside her and their windows open to the cold November night—this desire for fresh air no matter the temperature something they shared—Angelina was surprised at how much she loved hearing the chimes. Years ago, Will had asked for them, but she'd never gotten around to it. As she turned on her back, lightning flashed. After a few seconds, thunder. Then sudden and torrential rain. She glanced at the clock and was surprised a second time that it was so close to morning—almost six. The rain slowed. More lightning and thunder. Chimes. Heavier rain. Each force separate. She could see the dark trees bending in the wind. A rumbling, rolling vibration. Lightning and chimes. The rain shooting down, harder, stronger, for a second drowning out all other sounds. The thunder roared through as if it were splitting something apart, the house maybe. And Angelina imagined a crack starting at the front door and pushing right through the center of the bed. Then from a distance, the deep whistle of a train, half a one first, then longer, then three calls in a row. She imagined the train circling the house to give her as much time as possible. *Come on*, the train was calling through the storm. *Come on.*

CHAPTER 50

"With the panels upside down and in the wrong order," she said, "it's like a giant Mystic Square."

They were lying on their backs again, side by side, under a blue and white sky. It was a beautiful November day, with a warm wind. They were barefoot. Her hands were clasped under her head, and she was watching his billboard as if it were a TV.

"In their first life," John Milton said, "the panels were a blue and red ad for a Howard Johnson's. I'm going to miss them when I paint my sign on top."

"Lucy told me how she gave you crayons and index cards your first day of school. She said you always carried them with you."

He lifted up his lower body, reached into a back pocket, and produced an eight-pack of crayons and what she assumed were eight index cards. He pulled a broken piece of a black crayon, no wrapper, out of the box and held it under his nose as if it were a cigar. Then he gave it to her and she smelled it.

"Yep," she said. "It smells like a crayon."

"But isn't it odd how the different colors smell the same? And it's a moving smell—starting one place, ending another, disappearing until you inhale again." Which he did. "In between the start and the finish, the smell thickens—from candles to salty ocean with a spot of pepper and a spot of honey. I would recognize the smell anywhere."

"Let me smell that again." And when she did, she closed her eyes and inhaled the smoky, diesel smell, the rough speed of traveling far away.

"The cards and the crayons were so I would always be able to draw wherever I was," he said. "It made me feel safe. But I always drew on anything—walls, concrete, paper, cardboard. Anything except coloring books. Look, deer."

A whole family it seemed. Two bucks, several little ones. She heard a car in the distance. "Not many cars out this way."

"One or two a day is all." He reached his arms all the way back and then out to each side, one landing across her breasts. Then he put his hands under his head. "Lucy was like a magnet. Usually, I was going in all directions at once. But with one look from her, all the pieces of me pulled together. She showed me what I didn't even know was there."

"What will we do without her?" Angelina asked.

"She wanted to move out here with me so bad. But I told her no. I told her this was something I had to do by myself. She cried and cried. I should have known she'd figure out a way to get what she wanted." He sat up, staring at his billboard. "You can't believe how big the boards are. Even small ones like this are big. It's deceptive. From here, you can't tell." He burped and looked at her still lying on the ground. "I like looking at your mouth," he said.

The clouds were moving fast now. The sky still bright blue, but more wind more often. The weather was changing again.

"Tell me what you do when you're out on the billboard in the morning."

"I do a lot of things."

"Oh boy," she said, closing her eyes.

"My favorite billboard for morning is the two-sided one down by the old carpet mill. When I get there, it's dark of course. So I flip on the miner's lamp and screech the ladder off the truck. No matter how I lift it off, it always screeches. And my shoulder usually knocks into the red safety harness that hangs from the top rack, sending it spinning. I get my thermos of coffee and carry the ladder over and lean it against the steel pole that leads up to the billboards. Six steps on my ladder, then I move to the pole ladder."

"Why go to all the trouble of putting a ladder on the pole but not all the way down?"

"So it's not too easy," he said.

The wind blew her hair across her face, and she let it go.

"I climb up, and there's that moment when my head breaches the safe space between the two billboards." He turned to her. "*Breach* is another word I like. *Bifurcate* and *breach*."

She smiled. Birds flew high above.

"Then I crawl onto the catwalk."

Like a bear onto a ledge.

"The two-sided billboards are angled almost touching at one end and wide open on the other. Like teepees that got tired of standing and just laid on back for a bit of a rest."

"I never thought about it that way before."

"That's the same thing Lucy said. But it's clear as a bell for me— horizontal teepees. I camped out in one a few weeks ago."

"You spent the night up there?"

"It was on the ground. Which is unusual. We were installing the first digital billboard in North Georgia. The conversion took a whole week—and that's with getting weather-lucky. We had to drop the head, then cut the pole down so it could be sleeved with a stronger pole to hold the additional weight of the digital components. Then the electricians built the giant electronic screen and hooked it all up. Only one side of the billboard is digital; the other side is staying vinyl. One side the past, one side the future. Two heads looking in opposite directions."

Which was exactly how she felt.

"I hated to see the vinyl arrive. But now I hate to see it go. At least the vinyl was something real."

"What do you mean *vinyl?*"

"Like the material of a kid's inner tube or a floaty toy. When it's collapsed, it's kind of sticky. A compressed clump in a box. One of my jobs is to make sure each vinyl is folded in exactly the same way. So I have to start by unfolding it all the way out on the floor. It sounds like rain."

"What sounds like rain?"

"Unrolling it.

"Why does it matter how it's folded?"

"So we can all count on the way it will open out across the board when we're high in the sky." He looked at her. "But now there'll be no more folding—nothing to step on and nothing in my hands. With the digital squares, the only person who might need to go up there will be the electrician—and then only if there are problems. A computer will change the screens." He yawned. "But if I've learned anything from vinyls, it's not to discount change but to rub my face in it."

And he leaned down and rubbed his face in hers. And she laughed and laughed.

He sat back up and slapped his hands on his legs. "It feels like summer out here. But good summer. Lots of birds. No ants."

"I want more."

And he leaned back down.

Laughing, she pushed him away. "More stories. More about spending the night inside the teepee."

He sighed and straightened back up. "Late that night, the first night of the conversion, I drove back to the site and parked at the wide end, my headlights shining right into that triangular space between the two sides. From the truck bed, I pulled my sleeping bag, a pillow, a cooler, and a lantern. I ducked under the crossbar. It was so cool to be between the two faces on the ground—majestic and cozy, like the giant arms Lucy was always talking about. Or like being in a cave. I unrolled my sleeping bag just like a vinyl, only it was an unroll of soft rather than slick. I threw my pillow where my head would later be—in the apex of the boards. I scooted the cooler to one side and plopped the lantern on top. I kicked off my boots and dropped my jeans. I switched on the lantern, sat on top of the bag, and put my hands out to the side, to feel the dirt. Red Georgia clay. I grabbed a V-8 out of the cooler, popped the top, and took a swig. Then I pulled out my crayons and cards and made tiny signs."

Small lights in a triangle of darkness.

"Usually they only take the boards down to change the angle of the two sides or to convert to a larger head. Either way, a one-day project and we haul it right back up."

"It's like you live in a different country than I do."

He started to stand. "Back to work for me."

"Wait," she said. "What you do up there in the morning?"

"Damn, we got far afield." He lay all the way back down. "This does feel good, doesn't it? I'm almost as good on the ground as I am in the sky."

"So in the morning..."

"So in the morning, after I breach the safe space, I slide up the back, keeping my right shoulder to the board. With the small circle of light from my hard hat, I make my way toward the apex. No cars on the road at that hour. The only sound, my boots. I put my pack down and take my coat off. I sit between the walls of the two boards, letting one leg hang in the space between as I pull off each boot and sock. I stand again, my feet burning on the cold metal. Seems like it's always cold even in summer. I turn off my lamp and take off my hat. I make sure I'm adjusted to the darkness before I peel off my shirt. And—"

"You take your clothes off up there?"

"And then I drop my jeans. I never shake with cold. It's more like a wave into the cool air. I try to draw the damp particles into my pores. After a minute, I step out onto the point where the boards meet. By this time, in the middle distance, I usually see headlights—the first car of the day. And then beyond, if I've timed it right, which I usually do, I'm able to see the faint orange of the rising sun. Then I arch my back and stretch and piss out as far as I can make it go."

Angelina sat up. "You go to the bathroom up there?"

He laughed and stuck his hands under his t-shirt, rubbing his chest and gut.

"That is not what I imagined," she said, brushing twigs and pine straw and dirt and grass off her arms and feet and back and pants.

"Then I pull my jacket over and sit on it, both legs hanging high above the trees."

"You stay naked?"

"Cars start to sluice by beneath me. Another great word. I open my silver-topped thermos and pour that first cup of coffee, black as the sky still is above me. I save one mouthful of coffee for the full circle of orange—I swallow the second I see it."

"Every morning?"

"Just about."

"What if it's raining?"

"Then it's raining."

"Why do you do it?"

"To remind myself of the big picture and that I'm just one small bit of it. And to get the fun of it out of my system; otherwise I wouldn't be able to concentrate when I was working."

"I want to do it. I want to climb to the top of the billboard."

"Whoa there, Nellie," he said and scrambled up. "I don't even take Lady up there."

She began to trace the shape of his foot, then his ankle, and he closed his eyes as her finger headed underneath his pants and up the back of his leg.

CHAPTER 51

Will was finishing his morning walk, back on their street now, and he could see Mary Beth bent over, dragging a large box down her driveway to the street, her legs shockingly bare. He hurried to help her.

"Let me," he said, his breath visible in the morning air.

"Thanks, Will."

She straightened her short dress on her hips. Her matching jacket couldn't possibly be keeping her warm. When had women stopped wearing stockings?

"Angelina sure is lucky to have you around. My Bert is never home." She rubbed her hands together.

"Anytime, Mary Beth. Just give me a call. I'm glad to help."

He wondered why twenty-five years ago he hadn't fallen for someone like his neighbor, but he knew. He loved Angelina precisely for the odd jumble she was. When he'd set off for his walk this morning, she'd set off to exercise. And sure, Mary Beth would like having him around, but maybe he wouldn't want to be around in that case. It was a strange world they lived in.

He crossed the street just as the FedEx truck pulled up in front of his house. Will stood at the end of the driveway so Dale didn't have to go all the way to the door.

"Mr. Brooks, how are you?"

"I sure wish you'd call me Will."

Dale handed him the envelope and then reached into his pocket. "We had the twins' picture made for Thanksgiving."

Will put the envelope under his arm and accepted the photo. Two little girls—one blonde, one brunette, one in jeans, one in a dress—as different as could be, sat in a field of plenty—giant pumpkins and squash, a scarecrow. "They're looking so grown-up. Remind me how old they are again."

"Just turned three."

"I'm ready to have some pictures of my own to show you."

"I'm telling you," Dale said, hobbling back toward the truck, "being a grandfather is the greatest."

Will waved and headed for the house. As he was closing the door, the phone rang. His heart raced as he lunged into the kitchen to pick up.

"Dad?"

"Livie." It sounded as if she were next door instead of across the ocean in Paris.

"I'm going to stay here for the break," she said.

"You're not coming for Thanksgiving?" Will sank into a chair at the kitchen table.

"You said that was okay, right?"

"Yes, of course."

"Okay, well, I just wanted to let you know. So I'll see you all in a month for Christmas. My friends are waiting. Say hi to Mom."

"Take care of yourself," he said, his breath slowing.

"Bye, Dad."

"Livie!" he said loudly, standing up.

"Yeah?"

"Call if you can. On Thanksgiving."

"Sure, Dad."

And just like that, he was alone again. He put the phone back where it belonged. And he hesitated for just a moment before taking the bacon, eggs, and butter out of the fridge.

Three large empty cardboard boxes stood one on top of each other by the back door. He'd forgotten they had boxes to go to the street too.

He shut the fridge and arranged his breakfast ingredients in a line on the counter in the order he would need them. Then he grabbed all three boxes, each by a flap, taking them through the house and out the front door. After putting them next to the garbage cans, he turned to go back inside but stopped, looking up and down their split-level, part-brick, part-shingled house. He had liked it because the brick needed no maintenance, and Angelina had loved it for the way she could imagine the trees the shingles had been. This would be the first Thanksgiving they wouldn't all be together.

Because he'd wanted to hold it all one last time, he expected to feel as if something were broken, and yet he didn't.

Thanksgiving would still come.

A plane thundered high above. Mary Beth backed out of her driveway. A squirrel paused by the side of the road, then darted in front of her car. Will waited. The squirrel vaulted into their yard.

What if Angelina were not in the house? Well, of course, she wasn't. She was at the gym. But what if she wasn't in the house for a longer period of time? What if *she* were the one who wasn't going to be here for Thanksgiving?

Thanksgiving would still come.

They would have turkey, he told himself, heading toward the house. They always had turkey.

Right there on the front stoop he had to sit down. Wasn't that what his mother had said the fall his father left? *They would have turkey.* As if that would take care of everything. As if that would make everything normal.

He reached underneath him, grabbing hold of a rough brick. He knew that he could not always make everything okay. But he also knew he would never leave. The brick, which wasn't going anywhere either, felt cold and sharp. His mother hadn't been able to make his father stay any more than he could make Angelina stay.

Will remembered wanting Angelina to have everything she wanted, but that was back when one of the things she wanted was him. He hoped he was still one of the things she wanted.

He sat up straighter. *He* would cook the turkey this year. He pulled a weed that was sticking out from one of the cobblestones in front of him and stood. They would have cornbread too, he decided. Cara and Iris would love that. And it would make the house smell so good. Maybe he'd even take some to Stella. And what else? He wanted to re-envision the meal. He bet the cooking shows were preparing all sorts of Thanksgiving recipes this week.

On the front stoop, a black umbrella leaned against the house, and as he went in the front door, he scooped it up and dropped it in the umbrella stand. In the den, he turned on the TV, turning up the volume so he could hear it while he fixed breakfast. After all, he was the only one here. Then he set the channel to the Food Network, where a woman was arranging fall flowers for the middle of a table. They should have fresh flowers this Thanksgiving too, he thought. He would buy the flowers himself.

CHAPTER 52

The Monday before Thanksgiving, Angelina opened her eyes to darkness, wide awake with her heart pounding. Will was snoring unevenly. Four a.m. "straight up," as John Milton would say. She left the bed and pulled on jeans and a black turtleneck. She carried black socks and her boots out of the room, closing the door to a ripple of a snore.

Downstairs, without a light, she turned on the electric kettle, then went to pee. She gathered a thermos and a mug, tea bags. Moments later, she wrapped herself in her black coat and the long, multi-colored scarf she'd bought the week before. She felt for her gloves in her pocket, added her purse to her shoulder, cradled the thermos and half-full mug to her chest, and with her other hand reached for her keys off the rack.

When she started the car, the numbers 4:17 glowed yellow, along with other colors she was not usually aware of—reds and blues and greens on the dashboard. She left off the heat, not wanting to get accustomed to it. Twenty-three minutes later she was turning into John Milton's place. She slowed, not wanting to wake him if he wasn't already. She braked and cut the lights. Once her eyes adjusted to the darkness, she let the car crawl forward. She parked next to his red truck, put on her gloves, and as she reached to open the glove compartment for a flashlight, she spied her sea of umbrellas on the floor. When was the last time she'd even noticed them? And she was surprised, after all this time, to feel nothing except the need to get rid of them.

Out of the car, she balanced the door against the frame instead of closing it. She inhaled the dry November air, exhilarated by the dark, the possibilities, the stars overhead, the fact that the world right here right now was still thick with night and she was out in it. For too many years, she'd been afraid to crack herself open, afraid to look at the yellow. Afraid of what she would find and how she might need to adjust.

She climbed the hill, the flashlight close to the ground, carrying her thermos and mug wrapped inside the old plaid blanket she kept in the car. At the billboard, she turned off the light, again let her eyes adjust, and then stood there attempting to sense the presence of another person. She felt none. She stepped back and scanned the different depths of darkness. She saw no one. Relieved she was early enough, she took another slow, deep breath of the night that showed no signs of letting anything or anyone deter it. And then she spread her blanket at the base of the first wooden pole and sat with her back against it, her shoulders opening and dropping naturally, her body expanding. On this cold but not terribly cold morning, she turned her eyes to the glittery lights in the sky of this big world.

Soon the clank of a door shutting. She didn't move but worked to make out the shadow of the man she knew was approaching. A shadow that gradually filled in and also, the closer he got, began to glow—just as he had after Lucy died. He looked sparkly. Nadine, Lucy, and John Milton. In the darkness, she smiled.

He stopped in front of her. "I said no."

"But you meant yes."

"Damn," he said. "I did."

He held out his hand and she took it. Then he pulled her up and nudged her back against the pole.

She felt the stale warmth of his body—no covering up, no pretending.

He wrapped his arms around her and the pole, rubbed his rough cheek on hers, and lifted his head. "It can't be about sex now. It can't be about sex up there. Up there it's about something else."

She raised her arms, knocking his away in the process. "*That's* why I'm here—for the something else." Which she only just understood.

He coughed and spit to the side. "Let's go," he said, bending for the ladder, which he leaned against the front of the pole. "Give me your thermos."

She picked up her thermos and her mug, but he threw the mug off to the side. Then he dropped her thermos in his canvas bag, pulled his hat out and put it on, and hitched the bag over his shoulder. He grabbed hold of the ladder with both hands, and then released one and stepped to the side. She stepped in. Then he put his hand back on the ladder, enclosing her. She reached her hands high to a rung and began to climb.

She heard a small click, and light illuminated the steps. She could feel John Milton overlapping her a bit, her own shadow-net. Almost too quickly her gloved hands were reaching for the wooden ledge, which she crawled onto, placing her back against the board, then scooting twice to the right, keeping her hands on the ledge that was wider than she'd expected.

And then he was sitting beside her. The black sky seemed to be lightening. It was quite something to feel her legs dangling in unending space, no ground to reassure them or impose limits.

He took off his hat and his boots. Then he stood and stepped over her. She heard and felt him drop his pants and then his shirt on top of the pants. The ledge vibrated as he went to the end. Against the dark, the mysterious shape of him, his pee shooting into the air and landing somewhere below. Then he turned toward her, the ledge vibrating again.

"Did you ever make those drawings where you start with all different colors and then you cover everything over with black?" he asked. "You take the edge of a paper clip and scrape a design."

The table Will made for Cara.

"It's a sky like that," he said.

It was true. Fingernail lines of pink and orange and yellow appeared across the black sky. She slid up, her back against the board, and felt his hand around her arm. She took off her gloves and stuck them in her coat pockets. She unbuttoned her coat and he took it, reaching in front of her and dropping it to her left. Then he straddled her, his hands on either side of her.

An electric current ripped through her body. She shivered.

He reached to unbutton the top of her jeans.

"I want to do it myself," she said, reminded of those childhood—those pure—feelings of desire. She looked above his arms to the sky.

He stepped back.

She reached for his arm, pulling it around in front of her and stamping his hand onto the billboard. She unzipped her pants and pushed her underwear down with her jeans, pushing off her boots when she got to them, cold air swooshing up her legs. Leaning against the billboard, she raised her turtleneck above her head—she had not put on a bra. She leaned her whole body against the icy billboard.

He flattened his arm across her breasts, as if it were one of those automatic bars that click back against you right after the whistle, right before the ride begins.

She could hear his breathing accelerate.

"Not up here, remember?" she said.

"Right," he said, loosening his arm. "Do you want to pee?"

She shook her head, shivering again at all that was out here.

He spread their clothes underneath them and helped her ease down on top of them. Then he sat.

"The trick," he said, "is to relax into the cold, not fight against it."

She took a breath and tried to soften her body. She breathed out.

"Look," he said, "the sun."

She could see white light in the east with the faint beginnings of pink. Night handing off to day, the circle continuing.

He opened her thermos. "You didn't bring coffee?" he asked.

"Tea."

He laughed, poured some in the top of her thermos, and handed it to her. "I wanted you to come up here with me. It was a surprise to find out I wanted that. A nice surprise."

She wrapped her chilled fingers around the warm top. Then the rich aroma of his coffee drifted her way, and she wished she'd brought coffee.

"Cheers," he said, offering the top of his thermos.

She met him halfway.

"Before you rolled down the driveway," John Milton said, "I had everything I wanted—my own space, my own piece of land, my own billboard. And now it feels like there might be something else I want."

She turned to look at him, leaned her shoulder against his. "It's weird how that can happen—how a need can appear out of nowhere. Like a hole. And you aren't happy until it's filled."

"I'm best alone," he said.

Below, she could see the V of the trailers, Lucy's closing the top of the V, John Milton's on the north side, the empty one on the south. She could also see how high she was off the ground and leaned back, her head flush against the board. She reached down and grabbed the ledge. She had a shiver of fear, goose bumps like a wave across her body. "Maybe I could move into the empty trailer?" she said.

John Milton looked down and then out into the distance. "At school, the girls had coloring books, and I watched them add color to the pictures, carefully pushing the crayon in only one direction, staying inside the lines. I thought maybe Lucy couldn't afford those books, but one day at the grocery store, some coloring books were in the ten-cent buggy, and I had a dime in the pocket of my red pants. I chose one with farm animals. I'd never been on a farm. And I stood in line behind Lucy as if I were a separate person. When she saw what was in my hands, she asked me in a loud voice what I wanted with somebody else's drawings. I looked down at those chickens and roosters and pigs, then up at Lucy's chin to her blue eyes looking into my blue eyes. I understood something then. That the best drawings were the ones I made, the ones inside me, and I hadn't even known. She didn't have to tell me to put the coloring book back."

Angelina relaxed into the cold and looked out into the distance instead of down. Something else, that's why she was up here. So maybe it was excitement filling her insides, not fear. She wiggled her toes to make sure she could feel them. No lines. A blank page. What if? Across the sky, the pink light diffused and took on an orange cast, darkness no longer a cover for anything.

"It goes quickly," he said.

She was naked on a billboard, and her legs hung over the edge. A bird chirped twice from a nearby tree, then trilled. And then, a whistle.

"My very own train," John Milton said. "The world is full of wonder."

At that moment, a tiny arch of orange appeared in the east. The earth rumbled. The train's wheels on the track picked up speed. Now three long whistles, calling to her.

"Look." He pointed. "It's so cool."

The train emerged just under the rising sun, bits of silver through the trees. The whistles were loud and insistent.

"More?" He tilted her thermos toward her.

She held the cup while he poured, watching the steam curl into the air and disappear.

The wind sailed through and was off again, to stay in one place not an option. But then she remembered. "Thanksgiving is Thursday," she said. "What will you do without Lucy?"

"Miss her. On Thanksgiving, I'll miss her."

The colors of the sunrise arrived in layers and moved up in layers, but gradually became the whole sky. The whistles were fading but still there, and in their fading, she felt her urgency.

There was a beauty in the way she could count on Will and trust him. He was the rock she was about to crash herself against. She'd never loved anyone for this long, but she'd stayed inside the lines long enough.

"I'll be okay," John Milton said.

"I will too," she said.

More birdsong. All around them. She looked up and out, then back to John Milton. At his hairy legs. Hairy everything. When she arrived at his eyes, he was staring. At her face, then her breasts, then her stomach. She looked down too at the little roll of candy fat, relaxed into the space around her, and looked again. At the not-perfect person that she was. He grinned, and she smiled a smile that started at her eyes and spread all the way to her uneven toe. She tipped her head up and looked out at the mountains. She felt alive. And this time, the feeling was less shocking, as if it were getting comfortable inside her.

She turned to the north and looked out as far out as she could, slowly turning her head to the east, taking in all the world in front of her, the sun now a full circle all by itself, the day having risen. She continued past the sun to the woods on the south side of the property, all the way to the white and yellow behind John, behind her. She held onto the ledge and leaned out a little way to look back at the billboard. "Baby chicks?"

He spoke quieter than she'd ever heard him speak. "Soon after that day at the grocery, I made my own farm. I colored a sign with three baby chicks in a cage just like that one up there only smaller. At the top I wrote *Free Baby Chicks* like it is there on the side. The thing is, I can't remember if someone was giving the chicks away or if I was protesting for their freedom."

Angelina remembered an index card she'd seen in that shoebox. The picture on the front was of a little boy in red pants sitting on top of a blue mountain. The words *Free Love* floated in the sky like a cloud. Now Angelina wondered if those words had another meaning. Which gave her more goose bumps.

As she untwisted herself, a small bird landed on top of the ladder, and she startled. Brown feathers. White underbelly. A Wood Thrush, she thought. Or maybe those spots were the streaks of a Brown Thrasher. She stared into the round yellow eyes of the bird that turned in a hop to face the mountains.

We teach them to look where they want to end up.

From the bird to the shimmery mountains—as far as she could see. *What if...*

She put down her tea and pulled on her turtleneck. She started to stand.

"Looks like we might be bifurcating," he said, still holding his coffee.

Angelina smiled, slid up the billboard, and stepped into her jeans. After she eased back down, she stuck each foot into a boot and put on her coat. She crawled onto the ladder, but paused to look behind her, sighting the mountains sparkling in the light of another new day. Then one step at a time, she made her way down, re-sighting the mountains over and over again and letting each foot dangle in the air—just for a moment so she could get used to the feeling.

ACKNOWLEDGEMENTS

When I began to write *Love Like This*, my empty house was still several years away. In the fall of 2012, when our youngest left for college, I'd had children at home for thirty-one years. I finished this novel for *the first time* a few months later.

Huge thanks to Cal for his continuous support in a million different ways but especially while I was off writing. This book was what I was working on when I missed three New Year's Eves and two anniversaries. Thanks also for the careful editing and for making this time of the empty nest so much more than an empty house. Hooray, thirty-seven years and we're still having fun.

A special thank you to our children—Kathleen, Bobby, Jack, and Sam—for leaving home AND for coming back to visit, and to their partners in the adventure of marriage, Sam L., Claire, Taylor, and Katherine. Here's to the next generation of those who will leave home for great adventures—Mack, Lily, Wynn, Ro, Ruby, and McLin.

For a number of months, because I already had two novels in drawers, I tried to force these characters into a short story, but when I submitted that story to a workshop at Sirenland Writers Conference, the first thing Ron Carlson said was, "Well, this is certainly a story that wants to be a novel." Big thanks to Ron, and to Sirenland.

Thank you to Pam Houston for nudging this novel in the direction it needed to go—over and over again—and to PAMFA, this group of excellent writers from across the country, women who became friends and who were so happy when I finally started this manuscript after the one we won't talk about. For the feedback and the friendship, thanks especially to Karen Nelson, and thanks also to Tami Anderson, Kae Penner-Howell, Karen Laborde, Lesley Dahl, Heather Malcolm, Susan von Konsky, Katherine Ellis, Peggy Sarjeant, Patricia Smith, and Sarah Phipps.

Back in the early seventies, I had wanted to go to college in Vermont, but when it came time, I didn't even apply. I was happy to finally make it for grad school. Thanks to Vermont College of Fine Arts, and in particular to my advisors: Diane Lefer for her wild enthusiasm and encouragement; David Jauss for his attention to detail and his grounding in craft; Connie May Fowler for her creative sparks, especially the one that landed on Lucy; and Douglas Glover for insisting on things like plot and giving me opinions to disagree with. Ongoing gratitude to the entire VCFA writing community.

Thanks to Amandah Turner for the many reads and walks and to Missy Upchurch for sharing her story about the squirrel.

I'm grateful to the following people for reading an early draft: Robin Black, Katie Shea Boutillier, and particularly Jodi Paloni, who went above and beyond by creating an actual candy clock. Thanks also to Jay Schaefer who read a later draft.

Continued appreciation to the Ragdale Foundation, Writing by Writers, and Catching Days and its readers.

Thank you to the wonderful Vine Leaves Press, with special thanks to Jessica Bell for the awesome cover, to Amie McCracken for the cool interior design, and to Melanie Faith, who loved this novel from the beginning and who understood everything I was trying to do and who just may be my perfect reader.

Writing *Love Like This* was a journey into the subconscious. Scenes arrived like gifts in the dark of night, in the shower, while driving. Gratitude to all that lies below the surface.

READING GROUP GUIDE

1. Twenty-two years is a long time to do anything. Angelina is ready for something else, and so is her husband Will—only not the same thing. How do you measure the value in sticking with something versus the value in changing things up? If you have a spouse, do they feel the same way you do?

2. What do you make of Angelina taking her clothes off in Chapter 1?

3. Why do you think Angelina goes back to work once Will is home to stay? In Chapter 15, when her daughter asks how it feels, Angelina responds that it feels the same. What does she mean?

4. How do you feel about Lucy when you first meet her and does that change during the novel?

5. Angelina and Lucy make quite a team. Why is that? After the incident with the dead squirrel, what changes for Angelina?

6. How would you describe John Milton? Why is Angelina intrigued?

7. Both Angelina and Lucy enjoy candy. What role does candy play in their relationship? How does candy factor into Angelina's relationship with Will?

8. Let's talk about Will. Angelina does a good job enumerating his weaknesses, but he has a lot of strengths. What are they?

9. Houses, houses everywhere. Discuss the different ways Angelina, Will, Lucy, and John Milton relate to houses. In what unexpected places do houses pop up?

10. Families of origin are powerful influencers. How do we see that reflected in Angelina, in Will, and in John Milton? How do you see it in your own life?

11. In novels, sometimes place works to unite characters. Would you say that's true in *Love Like This*? Think of the porch, the billboard, the trailers, Best Buy, the headwaters of the Chattahoochee River, the gym, Running on Empty, the Blue Ridge mountains.

12. Discuss the role of water in the novel. What does it mean to Will? To Angelina?

13. In the first half of the novel, movies and other books are an important way that Angelina relates to the world. In the second half of the novel, Will mentions a book. What do these references add to the overall experience of *Love Like This*?

14. In Chapter 39, Will says, "They were a hub. Thanksgiving and then Christmas." Do you know what he means by this? What are Angelina and Will holding together? What is holding them together?

15. In this novel, there are two points of view. Did you find yourself siding with one spouse or the other? If you have a spouse, do you think they would feel the same way you do?

16. In Chapter 45, Angelina wonders "if up against different people we become different people." Do you think that's true? Have you seen it in your own life? Does it make you want to meet new people?

17. Are Angelina and Will good for each other? What about Angelina and John Milton? How does the book's title apply to these relationships? How does it apply to the other characters and their relationships?

18. From the boxes Will makes in his basement workroom, he's able to build a new vision for this time in his life. How does he do this and what else contributes to his new vision?

19. Over the course of the novel, what do Angelina and Will learn about each other and marriage? Did *Love Like This* change your perception of the possibilities of marriage?

20. At the end of the novel, what do you think Angelina plans to do? What do you think Will thinks Angelina is planning to do? What would you be planning on doing?

VINE LEAVES PRESS

Enjoyed this book?
Go to *vineleavespress.com* to find more.
Subscribe to our newsletter:

CPSIA information can be obtained
at www.ICGtesting.com
Printed in the USA
JSHW081242110123
36008JS00005B/16

9 780645 436570